Choices

Standing in the Gap or

Standing in God's Way?

Pat G'Orge-Walker

Done Deal Entertainment
Statesville, North Carolina

Choices Standing in the Gap or in God's Way?
Copyright © 2021 by Pat G'Orge-Walker
ISBN (trade paperback) 978-0-9660155-4-6
ISBN (eBook) 978-0-9660155-2-2

Edited by J.L. Campbell: JLCampbellwrites@gmail.com
and Lissa Woodson: www.naleighnakai.com
Cover Designed by J.L. Woodson: www.woodsoncreativestudio.com
Interior Designed by Lissa Woodson: www.naleighnakai.com

For permission, contact Pat G'Orge-Walker at Patgauthor@aol.com
234 Chestnut Lane, Statesville, NC 28625
www.pgorgewalker.com

Choices

Standing in the Gap or

Standing in God's Way?

Pat G'Orge-Walker

This book is dedicated to those who, like the Biblical Abigail, stubbornly cling to bad situations.

We, who believe we are standing in the gap, praying and fasting when we are actually standing in God's way.

Let go and let God. He wants to give you beauty for ashes.

◆ ACKNOWLEDGEMENTS ◆

All praises to God—full stop. My "hallelujahs" are nonstop.

Laying bare my soul wasn't easy. Prayerfully, God had several rams in the bush. I am eternally grateful to:

Shawn Williams for reminding Naleighna Kai of her vision for the Merry Hearts series.

Naleighna Kai - my Editor and Literary Agent. She orchestrated the Merry Hearts anthology as God led her to its successful end. Without her, this series would have remained an idea on paper only.

Stephanie M. Freeman's powerful foreword opened my soul and carefully extracted what made me—revealed God's intention, His purpose for my being.

J.L. Campbell. She holds a special place in my heart. When illness struck me, she latched onto the vision for my Choices story, editing and praying it through.

J. L. Woodson of Woodson Creative Studio. From cover to cover, your amazing eye-catching designs have made presenting my books a blessing.

Anita Roseboro-Wade, Marze Scott, Unique Hiram, Solsire E. Felida, and many others from my amazing and prayerful Naleighna Kai's Tribe Called Success family, for loving on me as I painfully made it to the finish line.

My beta readers, D. J. Mitchell and Kelsie Maxwell. Thank you for your honest critiques and comments. You made my heart glad.

I remain eternally grateful for the years shared with my late husband, Rob. He was my beauty for ashes.

Pat G' Orge-Walker

For every flower that grew in His garden, there was a seed. Some fell on good ground and their blossoms have their splendor. Others rode the wind and bloomed elsewhere to bring His message to the lost or fallen. And then, there are those with darker petals. They endure the bitter snows and blistering heat of adversity. In due season, nourished by the fertile ground of experience and a source everlasting, they too bloom. She is a rarity. Her color grows more radiant through the years. She nourishes the seedlings beside her from a well of hard-won wisdom. With leaves of green and veins of gold their dark beauty is unmatched and so is her story.
--Stephanie M. Freeman, author of *Necessary Evil* and *Unfinished Business*

Abigail & Nabal

Abigail and Nabal's marriage had all the necessary ingredients to fail or succeed. One spouse was self-serving, greedy, and unwise. The other was thoughtful and meticulous, in timing, despite being married to a "fool".

Abigail stayed home like a good wife, and when strife came upon the family, she never hesitated to draw wisdom from her mental arsenal, putting it to good use. She played it straight down the middle and made everyone happy. When Nabal, her husband of means, did something stupid—which had become a habit—it was Abigail who tried to keep order.

When King David protected Nabal's fields and homes from the enemy, ensuring not one stroke of bad luck befell him, he asked one thing of Nabal. "Can my army and I rest for a while? We have fought for you and your property and are tired from battle."

Nabal thought more of himself than he should have, probably assuming King David was too weary to do anything about the situation. He told King David, "Not my problem. You handle it."

King David gathered his weary soldiers and sent word that when he was finished with Nabal there wouldn't be a soul left to mourn, a blade of grass or building left to feed the hungry or provide shelter from the elements.

The story of Abigail and Nabal is one that connected with me the first time I read it. Although not a lot is known about the couple, one thing was for certain—Nabal was a fool and felt no reason to hide it. On the other hand, Abigail loved peace and used wisdom to neutralize messy situations. In the end, when Nabal's actions put her and the people she loved in fear of losing their lives, she was given a reprieve. Nabal died when God struck him, and Abigail eventually became one of King David's wives and lived happily ever after… finally.

Chapter One

Seven years ago, Anna was single. Single and happy serving the Lord. Her Harlem, New York-based church was her refuge, and at age nineteen, without any close family for support, the church filled that void.

That year, most of the single women in the congregation were either preparing for marriage or getting pregnant, hopefully after marriage or they got a ring. Anna was one of a handful from the one hundred members who had claimed neither. "I got Jesus, and He's enough," was her anthem. It didn't mean she didn't date on the side. It did mean that she would never testify or let the church know she did, especially the Church Mothers.

And then, as if a bolt of lightning had struck, the Mothers Board realized Anna had avoided the continuous Matrimonial "Sadie

Hawkins" day event. During one of the evening services, a visiting Prophet called for a five-dollar prophetic line. Anna did not have five dollars. If she had, she wouldn't have stood in that particular line anyway.

In her mind, only the visiting Prophet would make a profit, and it was hardly worth her while to subtract from her meager earnings. She was already indebted to paying tithes.

However, on a Thursday night during one of the fifty-two weekly Building Fund Revivals, Nabal Miller stepped through the doors of her church for the first time. He wasn't hard to miss in a congregation where women of all ages, shapes, and financial situations outnumbered the men by ten to one and a half. The half meant a couple of men were still on the "We ain't quite sure about brother so and so, list."

Anna recalled something exotic about Nabal that made the congregation pay attention, especially the Church Mothers. There were whispers that evening. "Who that? He looks so handsome. We ain't seen too many men with pretty gray eyes and that butter complexion."

Heads of dyed-black, and sometimes shades of light blue or purplish hair, covered with white crocheted crowns, popped up like bobble-head dolls in the pews. The women had buns pulled back tight enough to make their faces look ten years' worth of Botox younger.

The feverish offbeat rhythm of the drums chimed in with the rapid clang of tambourines. The clamor covered the spirited and fleshly words of admiration spreading from pew to pew.

"Y'all see that army uniform? My, my, I wish he'd keep my 'Southern country' safe," voiced several of the thirsty 'somewhat saved' women.

No one had a clue that the crisp green uniform with all its medals, his high yella, freckled face, and large gray eyes hid the real man. Not even the spiritual "God-done-showed-me-everything" women had seen it.

However, somehow that same night, one of the Church Mothers, according to her, experienced a sudden visit from the spirit realm. "The spirit showed me that this man is gonna marry one of our young sisters," Mother Mayhem propha-lied.

No one was more shocked than Anna when out of the blue, she heard her name called. She was already in a secret pre-engagement relationship with another young man from one of the sister churches. He hadn't proposed yet, but she knew it would happen. On more than one occasion, they went too far with groping and teasing, and came close to fornicating. Perhaps, God had shown that impending embarrassment and sin to the Church Mother.

One of the first things Anna learned when she joined her church was obedience. Obeying the Bible was something to strive for; disobeying the church elders, especially the Church Mothers, was a no-plea deal that led to eternal punishment in Hell.

Two days later, during one of the choir rehearsals, she overheard someone mention they had seen her secret 'friend' suddenly appear in Baltimore, Maryland over that past weekend. "Looks like that brother will be coming up under a new ministry," the person added.

Anna wasn't a genius, but it didn't take one to figure out it was no coincidence that within that same time frame, the Church Mother had convinced her and Nabal, God wanted them to marry.

She thought her and God were tight enough that He would have at least given her a better heads up than the sudden disappearance of the young man she wanted to marry.

Anna would never forget how those Church Mothers went into

overdrive trying to get her hitched. She felt like a bounty was on her head, and they were dead set on getting it. They insisted, "because the Lord said so." She did not have time to buy a gown or even something white or off-white. Getting married in January in New York made it almost impossible to find anything white.

The fear of going to Hell for disobedience was reason enough for her to do as the Church Mother prophesied. Nabal feared he might never return from Vietnam, or would come back a disabled person, so what did he have to lose?

One of the Church Mothers insisted the ceremony be in her tiny one-bedroom apartment. "Begin small so you can appreciate the increase," she claimed.

While they chatted, prayed, testified, and gossiped or "shared" as they called it, the Church Mothers hurried around the small kitchen where they prepared the wedding feast. The menu consisted of crispy fried chicken and dirty rice for the main course, and Communion wafers substituted for the bread. The food was greasy and served on two-ply paper plates. The wedding cake was a two-layer pineapple upside-down with a pair of small candles where a bride and groom usually stood.

Of course, Nabal wore his uniform with an assortment of medals, none of which she bothered to ask how he earned.

Anna wore an ugly blue and brown plaid suit. She wore her long, auburn hair plaited in a thick braid that hung midway down her back. Mute and rigid, her large brown eyes vacant as though she were having an out-of-body experience. A few of the invited church members and several 'who just happened to be in the neighborhood' milled around and waited while she stood, vulnerable before a preacher and a groom she didn't know, both preapproved by the Church Mothers.

Every detail of what she imagined her wedding to be was absent from this "sham" of a wedding ceremony. She was an angry bride who would become an angrier wife. Each time she watched a wedding, whether in person or on television, she grieved for what she lost.

The grief was compounded because she hadn't listened when she'd last spoken with her estranged father. They'd never seen eye-to-eye over many things. If she wanted to go left, her father insisted to go right.

Nothing had changed. As soon as Anna told her father she had married a serviceman, the negative analysis began.

"What makes you think this man is reliable? Where is his family? Didn't you feel that we would've wanted to meet them before you married? Other than you saying you met him at church, we know nothing. We would've learned something about him, but you married so quickly, we didn't even get an invite. He will not be the same when he returns from war. No one ever is."

* * *

Less than two months later, Nabal prepared to ship off to Vietnam. Anna wasn't ready to go through her pregnancy alone.

Not one of the Church Mothers offered advice or prayer that made sense. After all, they had done the first part. Their absence of caring showed she would have to figure out the rest on her own.

Anna did not want to be pregnant with a baby and with anger. How could those two feelings coexist? With her emotions in free-fall, she didn't know who to be angrier with. Nabal? Why not him? He could have said "no" to being forced into matrimony. But then, so could she.

One of the Church Mothers, out of habit, quoted a scriptural remix and, for Anna, it was the final straw. "God said," she always prefaced her supposed prophetic gifts with those words, 'Let the wheat and the tares grow together,' you figure it out which one of you is the wheat and the other be the tare. You just make sure you two stay together until the Lord separates and judges you."

Chapter Two

No Peace in the Home

Outside her modest six-room Brooklyn, New York home, a ferocious thunderstorm tore through the block littered with Bible tracts on doorsteps and liquor bottles in trashcans. Several car alarms began a syncopated horn ensemble that startled twenty-four-year-old Anna Miller, while sitting on her sofa. She recovered quickly, closed her eyes, refocusing on what caused the turbulence in her mind while sipping a cup of hot Pekoe tea.

Minutes later Anna closed her living room curtains, as if doing so would shield her from the tempest outside, she bit her lower lip. Her long, mocha-colored fingers showed remnants of pink month-old dollar-store nail polish. Her pulse raced as she crossed both arms across her chest in a coffin-like pose. She bowed her head and silently prayed.

Lord, she began slowly. Between small gulps of breaths, she continued, You said, you would put a thousand demons to flight. Lord, can't you rid me of just this one?

But who would help her if she never confessed to the truth? Who would help her when she was too afraid to speak hers aloud?

Anna had her reasons, or at least what she thought were good reasons.

There was a time in her past when she had been frank. She had no filter. She was brash, and whether it was necessary or not, someone's hurt feelings didn't matter. Nowadays, she feared repercussions, real and unimagined from a source meant to protect her. She was the Biblical rib of a man, her husband Nabal, without a heart.

Moreover, on the few occasions they did attend, how would her church members feel if she disclosed her nightmarish predicament? She was very cautious in front of the congregation. As had become her habit, she chewed her lip and swallowed the venom-coated words that built in her throat.

However, there were a few times when a congregation member mentioned how they noticed a change in Nabal. "Poor brother Nabal, I guess he gets a bit nervous with us playing the organ so loud and slapping away on our tambourines," the comment would begin. "Nobody expects him to be the same as when he left. I've noticed him a time or two, balling his fists instead of stretching out his hands to the Lord. But I ain't gonna judge him."

The one saving grace for Anna was Sunday School. She was happy her children, Diane and Marie, could enjoy the company of children closer to their age. They rarely had an opportunity to interact with other children when they were not in church. With them inside the small sanctuary where they sometimes watched a Christian children's bible story or played games, they could enjoy something that wasn't taught or seen inside their home.

However, once someone dismissed the service, Nabal would unclench his fists then quickly snatch Anna by the arm and lead her and their children out the door. As often as Nabal did that, she always wondered why her pastor and congregation didn't think it was strange enough to confront him. They did not have to judge Nabal, at least counseling might've worked.

The church was once her refuge; a place where she could lay sprawled at the foot of the altar and cry out to God. According to the Elders, God always heard her prayers, but God's timing was unpredictable, even though they sang, "He's An On Time God" before every Testimony service.

Anna had attended that same church since she was nineteen years old. She was once eager, God-fearing, and a part of the Street Praise team.

In those days, Anna stood on many Harlem, New York, street corners. She wore no makeup but dressed modest in the church uniform, an all-white, ankle-length dress. Her clothing was a sign of holiness.

She would smile and nod at the many rushing passersby before asking in her sing-song scripted approach, "Have you met the Savior Jesus? Follow him before it's too late. John 3:16 is your refuge."

Chapter Three

KEEPING UP APPEARANCES—OR NOT

Anna fished several bobby pins from a torn pocket of her faded flowery housedress with a half-sewn hem that was far from the neatness she once displayed. She was five-foot-six in three-inch heels, but hadn't worn heels in several years, not even to church.

Pinning several loose strands of her coarse dark brown unkempt hair that fell over one eye, Anna whispered angrily, "I need a touch-up." She rolled her eyes again at her image. "No room in the budget, I'm sure." She frowned at her reflection in the hallway mirror then spun around and continued her practiced tiptoe through her home.

As she stood outside her children's tiny bedroom, Anna straightened her shoulders, took a deep breath, and whispered, "I hope they're still sleeping." She believed that no matter what, a mother's lips should speak blessings over her children. It was the only room in her home where she didn't allow unhappiness, hers or anyone's, to violate the space.

Their father rarely entered, and she was grateful for that.

Anna was creative when decorating her home. "Vintage-cheap." Everything in her house had been inside someone else's before. She had decorated the room with pictures of hand-drawn, happy, fairytale characters. It hadn't been easy, but somehow, she managed to glue large, rainbow-colored alphabet letters onto cardboard. She made sure the cheap, stained cardboard would not show through. Everything on the bedroom walls was something educational. "The more you know," she whispered into one of daughter's ears. "The better off you will be. I'm gonna make certain of it."

Diana was four years old and the eldest of the children. Her daughters would one day understand the importance of those words. Anna would see to their happiness, and she would hurt anyone in her way.

Within minutes of ensuring that her two daughters were tucked safely in their bed and crib, Marie stirred. Anna's smile grew as she gently lifted three-year-old Marie from the crib. "C'mon Marie, let's get you a pretzel treat." With Marie out of the room, if she cried, Diana would not wake.

Anna continued her mission. Maneuvering the narrow hallway proved difficult, especially when she had to pause every few steps to adjust the toddler cradled on one hip. My goodness, Marie, you are getting so heavy.

Those same hips, at one time, were a sturdy but slender asset and served Anna well when she modeled for a women's sewing pattern company in her youth.

There was plenty of room on her hip, now a perch where she carried the squirming toddler. "Be still, Marie," Anna murmured as the child's wiggling increased. She kissed the infant's soft pouting lips. "Hush. We don't want to wake Daddy." Please don't wake daddy. Anna's steps quickened, eager to reach her destination.

Once she made it to the laundry room, after stopping in the kitchen and giving Marie a pretzel, she inhaled until her cheeks appeared sunken. Nabal came up with the idea to have the small laundry room in the rear of the house and refused to hear otherwise. Over time, she realized the more she and their daughters stayed out of his sight, the better he acted.

It could be different, but she hoped that if she avoided him, she and the children would be safe.

* * *

More than five years ago, Anna's husband, Nabal, returned from fighting in Vietnam. The transformation from good to evil, or unstable, was swift. Her ordeal began the same day he hung his uniform in the hall closet. "Out of sight, out of mind," he snarled before he threw his service medals in the back of their bedroom drawer.

Nabal had slumped on the bed with his hands clawing at the front of his pants as the new war had moved to his home front. He narrowed his eyes, then wagged his finger at her. "You tell anybody else how much you missed and loved me while I was away?"

Anna's survival instincts pushed the answer from her mouth. "Always," she lied, further evidenced by how her mouth remained gaped, and the jitters in her stomach.

"Tell me, where are the letters I sent you?" he demanded before flinging several papers off a nearby table. Again, his gray eyes appeared to darken like distant storm clouds as they swept the room, and he scowled.

Anna remained silent, but seconds later, she raced to a file cabinet in the corner of the room. Fetching a small black pocketbook from inside one of the drawers, she then untied pink ribbons wrapped around bundles of Nabal's letters. All the envelopes with their red, white, and thin blue lines running along the side, postmarked with an Army seal.

After giving him the white envelopes, Anna lowered her eyes and backed away. A few letters carried tear stains, a reminder of the worry after a time without a word, and then the mail arrived.

Nabal scanned several letters, turning them over in his hands as though checking for fingerprints or something wrong. He nodded and sighed. "You don't need these. I sent them 'cause I wasn't too sure I was coming back. I'm home now, so toss them."

Anna's pulse raced as she watched him do the unimaginable.

He did not ask if the letters meant anything to her; instead, Nabal ripped several envelopes apart with one attempt. Until that moment, she had not realized how physically strong he was when he wasn't raining down punches upon her body.

Every strip of paper that littered the floor erased all the undying love he had declared for his unborn child. Not one letter held any expression of his respect for her doing the necessary work without help from him.

Even then, Anna found excuses. "I didn't expect he'd come home and be happy twenty-four hours a day."

There were explanations, and then there were choices.

However, it did not take long before she ran out of justification for Nabal's erratic displays. Many times Anna walked into the room he occupied, regretting that she had.

Often, whenever a television news channel broadcasted updates about the war, Nabal's reactions became violent. Sometimes, he sat and rocked with his shoulders slumped. With vacant eyes, he would stare at nothing. Other times, with open palms, he would pound both sides of his head. His tears would stream. Then like shutting off a spigot, the tears stopped. Whatever he was doing before his meltdown, he returned to it as though nothing had happened.

For months, Anna witnessed his decline, and despite knowing better, she was sorry for him. She hoped he simply needed time to readjust to civilian life.

However, Nabal's readjustment evaded both himself and Anna. Whatever was needed took a long, scenic route. Nothing got better, and "worse" became the third entity in their marriage.

Anna struggled to learn the where, when, and how of Nabal's moods. She soon came to know that one sign.

"Can't you see I'm trying to concentrate?" Those words preceded a violent mood change. Sometimes, there was a follow-up. "Shut Diana up, or stop Marie from crying before I do it."

Anna couldn't determine the day or the hour when she realized, and much worse, accepted her reality. She and her children had become the enemy in their home. Neither she nor her children knew the rules of a war they had not enlisted to fight.

Chapter Four

DIMINISHING CHOICES

Before Anna met and married Nabal, she worked for two years as an administrative assistant inside Brooklyn's 72nd Precinct. On the same day Nabal left to deploy from Fort Knox, Kentucky, she learned she was pregnant. Diana was almost three months old when he returned stateside. With her thick dark curly hair, sandy complexion and gray eyes; she was the spitting image of Nabal.

Becoming a married yet single mother gave Anna a new sense of urgency and protectiveness. A Supermom. She felt she could do anything for herself and her baby.

By the time Nabal returned home from the war, she had already saved enough to put a down payment on a home, and Anna hired a babysitter for Diana during his absence. She was happy and eager to return to working her nine-to-five, never missing a day at the Precinct.

Almost as soon as Nabal returned home, Anna became pregnant

with their second child. Despite little sleep and relentless morning sickness, perseverance prevailed. Anna continued working.

Marie was born just six weeks shy of Diane's first birthday, with tight sandy-colored curls, and a rose-beige complexion, looking like a miniature Anna.

Anna had no choice but to stop breast-feeding after a few weeks and return to work. She worried about Nabal feeling less than a man and even though he made their marriage difficult with his mood swings, she still offered excuses for him. It was not easy for a returning Vet to find a job, she thought, so she did what was necessary to provide support.

Anna's choices diminished. The more she sacrificed, the more dreams she surrendered.

* * *

Without asking her input, Nabal took a chance on realizing one of his dreams and applied for a Veterans Administration loan.

"It finally came through." Nabal's smile was broad when he announced to Anna one Saturday morning, "It couldn't have arrived on a better day." He laughed and pointed to the living room window. "Sun shining on the outside and inside this house," he continued. "Now, finally, it's on me."

"What came through?"

"What do you mean, what came through?" Nabal spat as his heavy eyebrows formed a crease almost covering his droopy, tired eyelids. His laughter took flight, then he added, "Do you ever listen to me?"

Anna assumed her regular stance. She hung her head while her gaze pierced the tiles, giving them an evil look; the one she reserved for Nabal but could never deliver. Surviving had become second nature, so was lying. She knew his ego would accept her excuse. "I want so much for you, but I wasn't sure what it was you received."

He outlined his plans. It took a few months, but Nabal's dream of owning a trucking company became a reality. Despite its rocky start with a small list of clients, the venture eventually proved successful.

Anna appreciated the seldom felt happiness in her spirit whenever Nabal was in a good mood. Although things were not perfect, and even with his few flashbacks, she still received the mental and sometimes physical scars along with them. She held onto her optimism. After all, she still had her job, and that was her salvation.

Although the trucking business grew faster than expected, after she gave birth to their second daughter, Nabal ambushed Anna one morning in the living room as she dusted and straightened the doilies on the coffee table. "I gotta talk to you," he told her. "I got an idea."

Anna, accustomed to his erratic ideas, was thrown for a loop that day, and she sat on the sofa, anxious to hear what he'd say next.

"I need you to do for my business what you do for the people at the Precinct."

"What is that?" Anna smiled, thinking Nabal finally planned to involve her and whatever knowledge she had in the business. He needs me. He finally needs me.

"I know I told you to pay that babysitter out of your check," he began. "I done invested all my money in this trucking business."

"Yes, you have. God has blessed us," Anna confessed. She smiled at the thought of Nabal acknowledging that she could make a contribution.

"God ain't had nothing to do with it!"

No sooner had Nabal spewed words Anna would never say, than

she began clawing at her arm with a jagged fingernail. The peace she felt seconds ago fled without even so much as a goodbye.

Anna gathered her wits and decided to retrieve her peace of mind. Having harmony for the sake of her two children was as necessary as the air she breathed. She took a deep breath but said nothing.

"I can't keep trying to keep these books, oversee my workers, and drive the truck," Nabal complained.

"Can I help?"

Anna regretted her words as soon as the last syllable leaped off her lips.

He splayed his legs and placed a hand on his hips. He pointed his finger at her. "Why would you ask something so stupid?"

She quickly tipped her head back and gave Nabal a questioning look.

Nabal threw up his hands before he asked angrily, "Ain't keeping books and office work what you do down at that Precinct?"

Again, Anna did not reply, yet hoped her quick smirk went unnoticed. *What does that have to do with this?*

Nabal suddenly snatched a pile of papers from the gray metal desk that subbed for his office. He waved them in front of her. "City employee or not," he ranted, "You're quitting that Precinct job. I need you here helping me with all these statements and filing stuff.

"Filing stuff?" She did not want to confront him but felt it necessary to say something.

As if he had read her thoughts, Nabal snarled. "I don't know much about that part of the business. You know, and it's what you gonna do from now on."

Anna fidgeted with a loose strand of hair. The inner corners of her eyebrows lifted just enough not to betray her anger. *What was* missing was a plan. She needed to make a choice because she'd finally had enough.

"You ain't got a choice." As if he'd read her mind, Nabal pointed, adding slowly. "Besides, all that money you paying a babysitter ain't necessary."

He swung his head quickly toward the door. He stopped for a moment for reasons only he knew before focusing back on Anna. "I ain't trying to adjust my schedule no more. Me taking Diana and Marie for these checkups while you're sitting at a desk at that Precinct. It's too much. You had them. You take them." He sucked his teeth and pointed. "You give them a two-week notice or whatever it is they need. Two weeks, they can take it or leave it—or you can do the same."

As if little Marie agreed with her father, she wailed from the bedroom.

"Don't look at me," Nabal scolded. "You go and quiet her down so I can show you what to do with these truck logs."

Tears welled in Anna's eyes. She wanted to wail along with Marie. Little by little, Nabal was eliminating everything from her life that made her who she was.

Two weeks raced by, and Anna left the job she loved because of a husband she did not.

Lord, what choice do I have?

Chapter Five

Choices Have Consequences

Since leaving the Precinct, Anna's only contact with her old job was with a co-worker and friend, Alvina Charles, who was a thirty-five-year-old Anti-Crime detective on the job, but more like a big sister when off duty.

With ten years on the job, Alvina had a well-earned reputation of being divorced from an abuser. Many workers inside the precinct claimed her ex-husband was small enough to backstroke in a bottle cap and never expected it to work. Alvina was almost six feet tall in bare feet. At first glance, she favored the Disco Queen, Grace Jones, who had a hit song titled, "Pull Up to the Bumper."

"I divorced that male mosquito," Alvina would say angrily, "because he kept poking my kneecaps on his way up to where he should've started in the first place. That was mental and sexual abuse, and I didn't like it."

Alvina had one other reputation. On the job she would shoot first and never ask questions. Alvina's mission in life was to make every abuser pay.

Anna always laughed when Alvina relayed some of the misadventures she encountered on her dates. "You gotta admit, I am honest," she would tease. "I always give my fair warning speech."

"Which is?" Anna would ask, knowing what was coming next.

"I'm too trigger-happy." Alvina winked and added, "I'd shoot my husband first if he ever thought about hitting me or not declaring a 'No sexual satisfaction guarantee' before the marriage. My ex-husband taught me the lesson of self-preservation, and that education came with a degree."

As close as she was to Alvina, Anna could never tell how many times Nabal had knocked her down. Anna always knew Alvina would never understand the situation and why she stayed. After all, if anyone were to shoot Nabal, it would be her—his wife. So, the most she shared had to do with what was happening with her children; 'the girls', as she called them.

Anna hadn't testified about it at church either; it wasn't too hard to keep it from the congregation. Nabal had lessened her church attendance, too.

Anna chose to keep her misery between her and God.

Over time, Anna's thoughts turned angrier about leaving her Precinct job. At least if she were still working and making decent money as she had before, she could finally leave her disastrous marriage. Instead, she continued meeting Alvina for a quick bite at a burger place on the days or weeks when Nabal had his truck on the road. Even then, Alvina paid for the meals, although Anna had not asked her to do so.

She did consider asking her family for help. Her father had remarried and moved to Baltimore. They hardly spoke, and it was not her father's fault.

There were times when she wanted to pick up the phone and ask him to forgive her for ignoring his advice and concern shortly after she'd married Nabal.

She'd ignored her father, a man who was an ex-Marine who worked twenty-five hours steadily in a twenty-four-hour day. What did he know? War didn't affect everyone the same way.

Anna had chosen to concentrate on her new marriage and pushed aside her father's warnings, abandoning all further contact. When she reconsidered, Anna had also abandoned every notion about herself and what she wanted in life. That pattern began when Nabal entered, and it appeared it would end the same way.

"Don't forget today is the big day," Anna reminded Alvina during their chat on the telephone.

"How can I forget Diana's fifth birthday?" Alvina replied, "I haven't missed a birthday since my goddaughter was a one-year-old."

"You sure haven't," Anna replied as she adjusted one of the sofa pillows in the living room. "I always say you are the big sister I never had."

"Well, perhaps that's why Diana looks more like me than you. I'm so glad I didn't have a nickel in that Nabal dime." Alvina teased, "You can have the dime all to yourself and keep the change."

Anna ignored the shade Alvina threw and continued as though she had not noticed it. "Can you believe how time has flown? Anna held the phone away from her ear to listen in case the girls called out for her. "What time did you want to stop by?"

"Whatever time your husband won't be home." Alvina countered. "I told you from the last time he came in early off the road and found us laughing; he never makes me feel welcome."

"That's your imagination," Anna lied twisting the telephone cord. "He's just an introvert, and he seldom talks to anyone who isn't a part of his trucking business."

"Whatever," Alvina replied. "Besides, I'm just coming by to give my sweet little Marie a hug and Diana her birthday present."

"I can't wait to see you." Anna gushed. "It's been too long, and I need to know whose life you've made miserable by arresting them."

"You know better. Between you, me, and the usual wiretappers, I don't arrest. I shoot."

"Big sis," Anna laughed, "you are too crazy."

"Remember that and remind them that don't believe it."

"For instance, like who?"

"See you shortly, Anna."

As always, Anna smiled as she disconnected the call from Alvina. Smiling was something she seldom did since leaving the job. Taking care of Nabal's bookkeeping was not easy. She was confident that he kept some items from the Internal Revenue Service, but she remained quiet. Afterall, she'd never signed any of his tax filings and couldn't be held responsible. He had also decided that he wouldn't give her a salary but would provide an allowance. The allowance was for things that he alone allowed.

A short time later, after dressing them in their latest thrift-store couture, Anna ushered the girls into another room. They wanted to go outside to play. "No," she told them. "I can't watch you, and besides,

Daddy hasn't fixed your swing set, and you might fall. I don't want you to get hurt again."

Her concerns for their safety had increased almost to the point where she'd become obsessive.

Recently, when she bathed the girls, she found both had strange identical, bruises on their inner thighs. The shapes had indentations that looked like bite marks.

When Anna discovered the marks and what happened, she was shocked to hear them say, tearfully, "daddy did it."

Anna could not believe them. She would not believe them.

Nabal played with them so rarely, she reasoned that perhaps the girls had gotten hurt on the old seesaw in the backyard. She imagined maybe they'd slid a little too hard on the grips in the middle with their legs. A flimsy excuse, but Anna decided to accept it, although with some hesitation. They were children, and children imagined all sorts of things.

Yet Anna prayed. She poured out her heart to God because she wasn't sure if perhaps what they accused their father of might be the truth. The Devil is a liar, she told herself finally. No way that particular truth would set them free.

Some days, anxiety ruled her. Waiting for the next undeserved angry word caused panic attacks, and Anna turned down her plate and fasted. It wasn't too hard. Nabal sometimes did not give her the food allowance for the week. Depending on his mood, she waited for several weeks. His hesitancy to leave her with money usually coincided with extended trips for the business. "I eat more than y'all," Nabal would tell her. "I'll be back when I get back. Just make do." But there wasn't too much to "make do" with despite her effort to plan their meals.

Chapter Six

To Be Healthy or Not to Be

Over several months, despite not eating much, Anna still gained weight. She had diabetes, and her doctor had warned her of the consequences. "You have Stress-Related Diabetes, and if you don't do something about whatever is driving you and your blood pressure into a dangerous position, you are headed for an early grave."

Her unhappiness had attacked her body, and as much as she wanted to fight, she was mentally exhausted, and her cry whittled down to the one prayer she repeated often.

Lord, I know your word says that whomever you put together let no man put asunder. I'm trying, Lord. I'm trying not to let hate enter into my heart and marriage. Suppose it wasn't for my children,

Father—if it wasn't for them. Lord, I need to protect them, but I don't know how without making things worse for them. Father, please let Nabal feel some conviction for the things he does to hurt the children and me. We deserve better.

Anna had not yet added an "Amen" to her silent prayer before Nabal screamed her name. "Anna Miller, where you at?"

"Where I'm always at," Anna hissed under her breath. "I'm back in the laundry room," she answered loudly. "I just put in the last load."

Wiping sleep from the inside corner of both eyes, Nabal strolled out of the bedroom. He was disheveled looking, and his piercing gray eyes never blinked but remained focused on the wall behind Anna. Lately, the trance-like and lousy behavior had reappeared more often.

Anna gave no thought to her next move. She had a recurring role in Nabal's drama, and so, she flinched. Her eyelids fluttered as they swept the space about him. Please, Lord. Without thinking, she raised one arm to cover her face as she watched Nabal's fists become a blur. His fist pounded an open palm and accented each threatening word. "I'm-not-repeating-anything-I say."

Anna used every bit of strength she possessed to block a scream. In horror, she watched, transfixed at the transformation she had witnessed so often before that moment. Nabal's behavior morphed into something more frightening.

The change was quick, and she thought perhaps she had imagined his mood change.

But Anna had not, and within seconds, she was sure of it.

Then Nabal's body stiffened.

Move away, Satan. In Jesus's name, I command you, Anna prayed while watching his zombie-like stance relax. Thank you, Father.

Anna's words of thanks were premature.

Nabal shuffled his feet and his head jerked as though he wanted to free himself from the grip of whatever had him imprisoned. And yet, his behavior confirmed he was still unaware she was present or his children who were happily playing in another room.

Anna made a choice that was foreign to her. An option to survive this new menacing threat. She quickly, and with stealth, placed one foot in front of the other, each step in a straight path to the door.

"Hell, no!" Nabal's eyes rolled back into his head, and in anger, he pointed at a wall, barking as though he commanded an army. "Get back in line, soldier."

Anna did not know how long it was before she lowered her foot to the floor. Nabal's new level of crazy baffled her. She couldn't tell if his rapid hand gestures pointed at nothing in particular, or he was shooting at something he could not see but had to stop. Whatever it was, it chilled her to the core.

And then the trance disappeared, but Nabal's demon remained.

"You cook?" Nabal asked. Despite the returning of his normal state, he was still balling up his fists.

Anna wanted to answer but knew it wouldn't matter. He began gripping and tearing at the front of his pants. She recoiled as he kicked aside one of the children's toys before he rushed inside the bathroom. "It better be something on my plate when I come out. I ain't got but another hour before I need to pick up one of the guys. Make sure you pack something for the road 'cause," he warned, "I don't expect to get back here for a day or two. You gonna have to celebrate that child's birthday by yourself. I can't be here for that nonsense and on the road making money too."

Anna glared at his back. A sneer gripped her lips. They were movements she would never do in front of his face. Take your time. We'll be just fine.

"O kay. I'll ha-ve it read-y," she stammered.

She stopped on her way to the kitchen and peeked inside the small room where the girls often played. She found Marie lying on the blanket where she'd laid her, counting her plastic numbers. "Stay put." Anna blew a kiss Marie's way. "Mommy will be right back. You wait for Diane."

Anna then headed to the kitchen, feeling as though she was one of the appliances. Although she was always heated, he hadn't turned her on in quite some time. Like the refrigerator, she kept her cool when she could and rarely let anything spoil. Her self-esteem was the floor where Nabal stormed across. He never took the time to see if her heart or feelings suffered.

He reduced her to a cook and a waitress. Sometimes he made her cut the food into small pieces as though he were one of their children. Each time she cut those small bites of food for him it made her feel more humiliated. She could've chosen to poison each piece if she'd wanted. She'd lost count how many times she reminded herself that she was still a child of God, and that vengeance was His.

Under her breath Anna hummed the words from one of her favorite songs. It wasn't gospel, but she loved the lyrics to 'A Change Gonna Come.'

Tears welled from her eyes and thoughts, as she questioned God's timing. "Lord, where is my change?"

Yet, there had been a significant change among many. Anna was once a fervent daily Prayer Warrior. No matter where or how, every day at noon, she would whisper a prayer. She prayed not only for her and her situation but for others trapped in anything similar.

Time seemed to drag, and for the past six months, her prayers had turned into what she knew was against God's word. "Lord," she'd sometimes mumble, "I don't even care if that man has an accident with that truck. I'm tired of being a fifth wheel and ignored." Thoughts of Nabal having an accident with his beloved truck, or his second wife, as she called the vehicle, brought her a little joy and peace. Something, anything to keep him away or out of her life. A few times when those thoughts came, she repented. As time moved on, she felt overwhelmed and doubted if perhaps she was ever saved.

Whenever fantasies of maiming or wishing her husband dead entered her spirit and mind, Anna would repeat with conviction, "Satan, I rebuke you. You have no power over me."

After all, she reasoned, it had to be the work of the Devil.

Change came after many hours of watching her favorite pastors preach fiery sermons on television. More important to her were the moments she sensed a renewal and a return from her backslidden state. Anna embraced the power of the Holy Spirit that she believed she had lost. The sermons penetrated the shield she had held on to for far too long. "Lord, I know my cross is hard, but yours was harder."

She still loved the Lord, so she would never think such evil things on her own. It had also been evident to her that when she prayed, "Lord, thy Will be done," that it didn't mean God took her advice over what He had planned.

Waiting wasn't easy.

* * *

The sound of the toilet flushing brought Anna back to her senses and her current situation. And away goes my marriage down the drain. She forgot her treaty with God and how she would leave it to His will. She glared at her wedding picture on a nearby table.

"Begin with a mess. End with a mess," Anna lamented.

Every time she saw herself dressed in that two-piece plaid suit instead of a traditional white wedding gown, she wrung her hands and made a fist as though she could fight her past.

Why am I going to Hell or going through Hell— No matter what else happened, Hell was always on her menu.

More times than she could count, Anna tried to see things from her husband's point of view. It wasn't easy. How could it ever be? They were never on the good foot because they'd started on the wrong foot.

Chapter Seven

Time's Up

Anna had stood by and watched Nabal work on his dreams' success with an urgency that he should have used for their marriage. Anything she needed for her and the kids had to wait until his business grew. That was his excuse, and he never deviated.

"We didn't discuss buying new clothes, did we?" Then came the usual slapping with one hand against whatever piece of furniture or flesh that was available. "Anna, stop eating so much, and you won't gain weight," he'd snapped.

"It was just a dark skirt for the Revival next week," Anna explained. Her words lingered and had the tone of apology with each syllable. Now was too late to snatch the words back. Lord, please don't let him hit me.

Anna refused to cry out if Nabal followed through, assaulting whatever part of her body got in the way of his fists. She would not allow her children to see her cry. This was the one promise she always kept.

* * *

Her next confrontation with Nabal was different. Marie had managed to get off the playmat and come into the living room. She carried a small cookie in her tiny hands and showed it to Anna. "Some," Marie said as she lifted the cookie in the air again— her way of asking Anna to share.

"No, sweetheart," Anna whispered. "Mommy doesn't want a cookie."

"You, lucky," Nabal told Anna through clenched teeth. To Nabal's credit, if he were to have one, he never shouted or abused Anna in front of their daughters.

Nabal gently took Anna by her elbow and lowered his mouth to her ear. "Hurry up and put that kid back inside," he spat. "We ain't finished talking yet."

Anna moved quickly. She realized Nabal's rant that day didn't carry its usual harshness. She seldom walked away unscathed.

Those were the moments Anna feared. The times when Nabal was angrier and more vindictive than usual. The lapses between the War in a faraway jungle—and the imagined war he fought at home. A war where Anna was the enemy.

This time, before Anna could stop her, little Marie came into the room again. She headed straight her way.

"Stay right there, Sweetheart!" Anna cried, but Marie had moved too quickly.

Nabal snatched Anna by the end of the scarf covering her hair. "You gonna learn today."

He knocked her to the floor and threw several hard punches as Anna cowered over Marie, receiving blows that would harm her tiny body.

With every blow and curse word Nabal delivered, she folded in a fetal position with Marie tucked under her whimpering, Anna's breaking point had finally arrived.

At that moment, Anna made a "biblical Anna" decision. She'd had enough of that 'fool'. However, unlike in the Bible, she didn't have a donkey to ride off and make things better and safer for her children, but she did have the keys to their 1973 Ford Pinto, and it was close enough.

Marie's crying caused Nabal to regain his senses. He glanced down at Anna and Marie, then walked over to the corner of the room and kept carving a part through his hair. His normal yellowish complexion looked ashen, and his eyes bewildered, as they turned wildly in their sockets, like two moving orbs. He began shaking while searching through his front pockets before retrieving the keys to his truck.

Nabal threw one more glance at Anna. She had not moved off the floor, and she stroked Marie's face, trying to kiss her daughter's tears away.

"You made me do that." Nabal accused. "You always take me there."

Without a coat to shield his body from the chill of the rain that had begun a short time ago, Nabal raced out the door. He slammed it hard enough to break the latch.

As soon as Anna heard the sound of Nabal's truck starting up, she gulped a deep breath. Seeing that Marie was not physically hurt, she took her back to the other room and rechecked her legs, arms and the lower part of the back to make certain she was not harmed. Anna willed her body to stop shaking, relieved Diana was distracted and watching a favorite cartoon channel.

"In the name of Jesus," she prayed as she went to the window and made sure the truck was gone. "Father God, I can't do it. Please forgive me, but I can't do this anymore. He could've killed my child."

Anna tried twice before she dialed the telephone number she had called many times. "Alvina," she began as the tears poured, but couldn't continue as words failed to come forth.

"Anna, what's wrong?"

"Forget about Diana's party. Please come quick. Come get the girls and me." Between more tears that led to hysteria, Anna told Alvina everything.

Alvina's voice blasted through the line and quivered as she spoke. "I told you before. I didn't like him because he always acted shadily. I thought he just wasn't feeling me or didn't want you having friends."

"I was too ashamed to say anything," Anna confessed.

"Ashamed to tell me? Anna, whether you told me or not, you should've left that fool a long time ago, or worse."

"What's worse?" Anna asked, holding the phone under her chin while tossing a few things into a bag. "I have my kids to think about." Anna had regained her composure and resolved to get as far away from Nabal as she could.

"That's what I mean," Alvina snapped. "You wouldn't have to kill him. He's pissed off enough people that they'd form a line and do it. You'd be a happy widow, but your kids would be fatherless. Both situations are better than the one you're in now."

"You're right."

"Don't give me that 'two worded' answer nonsense. I ain't no church girl, but I swear, Anna, you always talking about Jesus, and me praying instead of cussing and fighting. But if you have prayed and you still get your butt kicked, don't open the church door for me. I'll take my chances with the Devil. At least he's consistent."

Anna had not realized that she'd stopped packing her suitcase. Alvina's words and the current situation smacked of all the truth she avoided or excused. How many times had she read the scripture that he who finds a wife finds a good thing?

Anna was a good thing. She was a good wife but one lacking wisdom. Nabal could've killed her and their daughters.

"And, speaking of church," Alvina continued, raising her voice as though it were her preaching this time instead of Anna. "Come to think of it. Didn't you just speak to me about that Bible story where there was a woman named Abigail? Didn't you tell me how she got tired of her husband putting his riches and selfishness before her happiness, or his workers and community? Wasn't it that Abigail who saved herself and her village from King David erasing them off the map when she humbled herself, took the King the best of her husband's belongings, and declared that her husband was a nasty, violent fool?"

"I didn't exactly speak on it like that—"

"Whatever," Alvina snapped, and Anna clamped down on the rest of her sentence.

"You and your daughters are the best that idiot of a husband had, and he didn't care. So, you don't have to ask me again. I'm gonna come and get you."

"Thank you." Anna's voice softened as she continued. "I'm sorry I upset you. I hope you calm down before you get here."

"Apparently, you have forgotten who I am."

"I haven't," Anna said, "I just don't want any more trouble."

"Heffa, pulleeze." Alvina snapped. "For you and the girls' sake, I'll leave my gun inside my car. So now, Fake Anna, what are you gonna do? Are you ready to stop this madness and save your family and your sanity?"

Anna's resolve strengthened, and she stood tall in the center of her living room. "Yes, I am."

"About time," Alvina barked. "Get your Anna-self-preservation self together. I'll be there in less than ten minutes."

Anna glanced around the home she had vowed to leave before she replied. "I will."

"And," Alvina warned. "If that fool returns before I get there, just act like you always act when he's kicked your butt. Shut up!"

Now, there was no turning back. Anna needed the wisdom and resolve of the biblical Anna. How many times had she read about the woman, Abigail, and never saw the similarities? She peered at the clock on the living room wall. It's two o'clock. That fool Nabal will be checking in on me soon to see if I got his things together for his road trip.

Anna had not heard her daughters come into the living room. Diana had Marie by the hand and was walking her carefully over piles of clothes and other things thrown around the room.

"What you doing, Mommy? Diana looked sad and confused as

she stared at several bags filled with clothes and toys. "You giving my stuff away on my birthday? Are you buying me new stuff?"

Anna stopped moving. She rested both hands on her hips and smiled, trying to appear more confident than she felt. "I had to make a choice," she explained that freedom would be their birthday present.

With a confused look on her face, Diana asked. "Why?"

"Because Abigail made a choice when push came to shove, and it worked out better than fine." Anna smiled, a real one this time. "It's from the Bible, Diana. You won't understand."

Diana released Marie's hand. She placed her hands on those small hips and reprimanded Anna. "Are you gonna do something that will make God mad? Mommy, you always sayin' how it looks like you be making God mad."

As Anna looked down at Diana, she was reminded of how she must've angered God when she hadn't confronted Nabal when she'd discovered the bite marks on the girl's thighs.

What a coward I am, she'd confessed. I promise Father God, I will never do that again. All that I am and will ever be is because of you. Forgive me, Lord. I will live in your Word, as well as never allow any man to abuse or hurt me and my daughters again. Amen.

For the first time that day, Anna's smile turned into laughter. "Not today," she told Diana finally. "I think I made God proud."

Anna felt a surge of power after repenting. A feeling she'd not felt in years. She was reminded of the night she received the Holy Ghost. The pain from the beating Nabal doled out had disappeared and was replaced with peace and joy.

Anna envisioned God looking down, wiping his brow, and saying, "Anna, it took you long enough to learn that I cannot bless a mess unless the two are equally yoked. You were such a hardhead, but

I'm going to give you beauty for your ashes. I know the plans I have made for your good. Jeremiah 29:11—"

While Anna waited for Alvina she lifted her bible from its place on the shelf under the picture of Jesus' Last Supper. She remembered what Alvina said earlier and opened it. With another sigh of relief, she turned to the Book of Samuel and began reading 1 Samuel 25:23-25.

When Abigail saw David, she quickly got off her donkey and bowed down before David with her face to the ground.

She fell at his feet and said: Pardon your servant, my Lord, and let me speak to you; hear what your servant has to say. Please pay no attention, my Lord, to that wicked man Nabal. He is just like his name—his name means Fool, and folly goes with him.

Anna had no idea where life would take her but was taking a breath of relief that this chapter of her life was closed.

Chapter 8

GAP: A BREAK OR OPENING/INTERCEDING

"To everything there is a season, and a time to every purpose under the heaven."   Ecclesiastes 3:1 (KJV)

The fictionalized story of Anna and Nabal's marriage was based, in part, on my first marriage. There were several incidences from it that mirrored my experiences. Giving in to my vulnerability and sharing it on the page wasn't easy. However, if you see yourself in a similar situation just know you are not alone.

Making a poor choice led to abuse. Deciding to stay longer than I should in a cult that triggered the same choice, could have led to my death.

* * *

Heart to Heart

Harlem, New York in the mid-sixties had everything for everybody. The world-renowned city wasn't known for colorful flowers in picturesque back or front yards. However, it didn't lack color, and was populated with a rainbow of complexions from light-bright to almost blue-black with attitudes to match.

Proper English was the language mostly spoken in downtown, New York. Pig Latin: a string of words and syllables sliced and diced to show how hip one happened to be was the secret and coded speech of uptown, Harlem.

After midnight, the Harlem mesmerizing atmosphere of illegal fun became catnip to the underground rollicking crowds of the sixties. When the sun went off duty and the moon came on, venues like the Cotton Club started jumping. Finger popping and grinding gyrations were performed by a crowd who leapt and hollered along with the hypnotic Jazz and Blues beats. In another room, scantily clad dancers were available for 'whatever one liked' for a price. They never gave their true names and didn't care to know yours, either.

Adding to the mix were many conked-hair-wearing, wanna-be playas who eagerly talked a good 'money-making game' while they hid one hand in an empty pocket. If talking "smack" was a paying job, they'd have been millionaires.

Harlem also had hundreds of churches. Many were squeezed in between the Po' Boy liquor stores and Bury Em Deep Funeral Homes, Inc. Some churches were pastored by those called by God. Others merely turned their collars around and purchased a brownstone.

The Brownstone preachers were the ones who hung tiny light bulbs shaped into a cross and scribbled a Bible verse on their "Open for Business" signs.

Harlem didn't discriminate. The wise and the foolish were offered the same choices. Rarely was the right one chosen.

I should know. The path I took was laden with wishful thinking and a desire to know that Jesus I'd heard about from my youth.

Leave it to me to pick my House of Worship, out of season and with no good reasons.

I lost count of how many times I wondered if Jesus was behind door number one, two, or three.

At the age of nineteen, I became involved with a church in Harlem, New York. I didn't know or realize it was a cult. The wearing of all-white uniforms, the starched crocheted white crowns along with marching orders to stand on corners and glean (beg) wasn't on my radar as a "clue." I was just happy to be a part of something. After a horrible argument with a family member who became angry when I dodged a cup of hot tea thrown in my direction, I left with no place to go. It wasn't my first time visiting the church. I felt comfortable testifying, so it seemed natural letting the congregation know how close I'd come to being homeless. They offered me a place to stay in one of the small rooms, which had a cot. How could I not be grateful?

Along my spiritual journey after I'd moved into the church, I made detours. Many roads I took were paved with "lacking wisdom" and straight highways of "willing to obey without questioning." Before I knew it, choosing the wrong paths took over, and my life changed, dramatically.

The women outnumbered the men about ten to one. The elderly, and/or the widowed, often played the role of matchmakers. They'd act as though they'd met with God daily to receive personal marching orders. Being the pious of the pious, no one questioned their authority to decide who married, when, and to whom. I accepted it like the other members because I never thought their marital decision would come around to me.

Years ago a strange wind of craziness was howling one Monday night in January. It carried into my space a situation I hadn't considered.

Several days passed before the head of the Church's Mothers Board interfered in my life, and that didn't just rock my world. Their decision sent it spinning out into the galaxy.

A young man appeared at the church and testified that he was twenty-one and about two weeks or so away from leaving for Vietnam. Although he wasn't very tall, in that full dress uniform, he looked like a giant. No matter how I feel about him now, I will confess, he did look good. I'll give him that.

The next thing I knew, three days later. You— Read —That — Right! One of the Church Mothers whose words, most of the time, began with: "Thus saith the Lord," or "God has spoken," stood and said God had shown her this young soldier named, Lee, and I were to marry.

Say what now?

Come to find out, he was no wiser than I because he agreed. Looking back, I can understand how, being sent to Vietnam without knowing whether he'd survive.

He never proposed. Instead, he invited me out to eat on the

upcoming Thursday night. Back then, I didn't turn down free meals.

A White Castle on Empire Boulevard in Brooklyn was located on a corner down the block from the famous Empire Skating rink. Sometime between a White Castle slider with cheese, greasy fries, and watered-down Coca-Cola, he slipped the ring on my finger.

Another clue? Another choice? Most definitely, but I digress.

Like the fictional story of Anna and Nabal, Lee and I were married in one of the Church Mothers' small apartment. I wore an ugly suit, and Lee was dressed in full uniform with medals. For some reason, I never found out how they were earned.

His tour of duty in Vietnam lasted a year and since I didn't know who he was before we married, I was introduced to the real him on his return.

The violence and the paranoia that should've been left on the battlefield came home with him. The sex was violent, demanding and those old, "I got mine— hope you got yours," sessions left me nauseous and resentful. Through all of it, somehow, three beautiful daughters were produced.

There was no expectation of him returning with a bouquet of roses in one hand and flowery words of praise falling from his lips. Those were the things he'd done and said during the two weeks of marriage before he left for Vietnam.

Sadly, after five years of being unequally yoked, his PTS—Post Traumatic Syndrome, became worse, especially the violence. I finally left to save myself and my children.

A close friend and coworker came to my home. A short time later I had the children in tow and left with only a suitcase packed with their clothes. That same day as he was arriving to the house, I was already getting into the passenger side of my friend Al's car. I cared nothing about the house and the bank account he'd already emptied. Lee was either too shocked to say anything or he spied the gun visible in Al's holster. Either way, I was leaving, and nothing was going to stop me.

I was fed up with being a punching bag. Fed up with being the recipient of his jealousy over invisible demons that, somehow, I'd welcomed into our home. In retrospect, I might've stayed, had therapy or counseling for those returning from, and dealing with, horrific war experiences, been available. Honestly, I'm not sure it would've mattered. Lee and I were two young people who never knew each other beyond our first and last names before being forced by my former church into marriage. Both of us understood even less of life with three innocent children, under the age of six, left to wonder what happened.

Years later, my middle daughter revealed that she'd always felt she'd must have done something wrong to "make daddy leave." Even now, I'm not certain she ever believed me when I told her she hadn't.

In some instances, however necessary, good choices are not readily understood or appreciated.

Chapter 9

"To appoint unto them that mourn in Zion, to give unto them beauty for ashes, the oil of joy for mourning, the garment of praise for the spirit of heaviness, that they might be called trees of righteousness, the planting of the Lord, that he might be glorified."

Isaiah 61:3 KJV

I should've known something was up when months after I'd left with the children, Lee began showing up unannounced, and against my wishes. Sometimes he'd drop by as though he were coming in from work and I was supposed to have something waiting for him.

One day, he came by and suddenly dropped his pants. He then asked would I sew a split he'd gotten in his material.

"You truly are crazy." I said, exploding with anger. "I'm not sewing anything, so pull those pants up."

When I refused, he cursed under his breath then warned, "You'll be sorry."

It wasn't so much that he'd said those words. I'd heard that threat before. Yet, that time, it was different and more resolute.

For weeks after that weird and threatening exchange with Lee, I became anxious, knowing what he was capable of and waiting for the other shoe to drop. When I'd finally reached a peaceful place where I no longer felt threatened, it finally did.

My fear became a reality, and the revelation happened on my birthday.

* * *

Instead of feeling happy on my birthday, misery set in and I couldn't relax. My daughters were away with their godmother for the entire weekend. However, Al, my rescuer on the day I'd left Lee and taken the children with me, called.

As my friend and bowling partner, he determined misery would not sully my birthday. By that time, I'd known him for almost two years. We'd met when I worked one of the token booths in the Bronx and discovered how much we had in common. We loved "General Hospital" a popular soap opera. At that time, he was married, and his wife was a former beauty queen. She was a huge fan of "All My Children", and I liked her from the moment we met.

When Al and Sheila divorced, I was not only surprised, but saddened. I felt like she'd divorced me too when I was no longer able to discuss confidential female issues with her. I never found out what caused the split, but if I placed money on it, I would attribute it to Al.

Al loved being a Transit cop. At twenty-nine, he'd been sworn in and now in his mid-thirties, he hadn't changed too much. He loved helping folk, but like the character Alvina, in my fictionalized Anna and Nabal story, he had no qualms about shooting, if it was necessary.

An avid bodybuilder with dark-brown, straight hair with not a strand out of place, Al was what we called, "the package". Everything about him looked good—starting with the way he stood six foot tall and erect, often with his hands clasped in front like a fashion cover model. That pose always drew a female's attention and at times, a few men. Every railroad station he worked resulted in new telephone numbers which he claimed with a smile, were for "further surveillance or interrogation".

Was Al overconfident? Yes, he knew it and always determined to let the world know too. He was just that handsome with a disarming smile used as effectively as when he pointed his gun. If the light-bright and almost white, R&B singer, El Debarge wasn't so skinny, Al and he could've passed for twins.

Although he was also my bowling partner off the job and remained a wonderful confidante on it, our friendship never went beyond the brotherly-sisterly realm.

Birthday or not, Al pestered me demanding to know what was wrong.

"Your birthday," Al began. "You can marinate in misery or tell me so we can get this celebration started."

Without reason, I began adjusting the blue jumper suit I wore. There was nothing to fix, but I had to use my hands for something or punch a wall.

"I've started again, probably for no reason, wondering about the threat Lee made some time ago." I tried to sound confident but failed.

Al threw up his hands, a move I knew meant he was about to share some of his always-ready-to-go wisdom, "Lil Sis, I keep telling you that when a man is overly jealous, threatening, and you know you've done nothing, the guilty one is him."

"So, you always say." I was too ashamed to look Al in the eyes. I'd lost count of how many times we'd had that conversation.

Al checked his watch before grabbing his jacket and hat. "I don't know why you had to be born in the winter. It's cold enough to freeze Hell."

"Blame my mama," I told him.

"Don't play with me. You know I don't know your mama." A smile crept across his face. "Listen, be ready by the time I get back. I need to pick up my present."

I lifted my chin, turned my head, then gave him a questioning look. "Don't you mean *my* present? Your birthday is in June."

Al opened the door to leave. "Mind your business."

Later that same afternoon, Al and his current woman du jour—his flavor for the week or his present—took me bowling. The two had a surprise birthday celebration for me, attended by seven members from NYCTA (New York City Transit Authority). I was able to relax for a moment after we'd won several games.

After all the bragging and my acceptance of the winning trophy, Al and his girlfriend drove me home. The feeling of elation dissipated as I sat in the backset with my mind elsewhere.

My attention returned when I caught Al looking at me through his rearview mirror. "What's up, Lil Sis?"

"Nothing," I lied. And that bothered me. I never lied to Al. He was the keeper of my secrets, and my backup, should the Devil decide to act up.

"I know you. We shall chat later."

In the rearview mirror, Al's lips were tight and that 'worry mask' remained. "I don't know how many times I need to tell you to stop accepting punishment from an ex, who I bet used you as an excuse to step out." His voice raised over the humming of the car's engine. "He's gone. Good."

During Al's outburst, from where I sat in the backseat, his girlfriend, seated next to him pulled down the front visor pretending to check her makeup. In the mirror, she met my surprised gaze. She turned her head aside and threw a questioning look his way. He ignored her, but I guessed his intention. Whatever Al had planned to do with her after he dropped me at home was cancelled.

* * *

As if Al had been forewarned when we went bowling for my birthday, the proof of his insight was in my mailbox that same day. A letter informing me that because I'd not fought the previous divorce filing notifications, a date was set for the proceeding. Although, my name and non-acceptance of previous notifications were returned to the court, stating I had "abandoned" our marriage and he had remained "faithful", I didn't fight it.

Soon after the divorce was finalized, I learned Lee had a son who was a little younger than my youngest daughter. Didn't shock me. He went on to have a daughter who was also a little younger than our youngest child. As Al had warned on several occasions, it appeared my ex-husband had stepped outside our marriage on occasion and punished me instead of accepting his guilt.

* * *

It took almost two years after my divorce, before I found my footing and had already joined a new church in the East New York section of Brooklyn. Fortunately, two years before my marriage ended, I'd begun working for the New York City Transit Authority as a Token Booth clerk. I sold tokens primarily along the "A" and "C" lines in Brooklyn, New York. The money was decent, and I had a steady babysitter for the children. Housing wasn't a problem. The two-family brownstone was returned to me along with a very small child support stipend; one that wasn't paid and that I refused to chase after.

One November night while working the Rockaway Avenue "A" line train station, several Anti-Crime cops came on duty. They were stationed inside and out of my booth. I had lost quite a bit of weight since eliminating the excess torture from the marriage. My self-confidence had returned. It was good to feel feminine and fine again, and I rarely wore the same thing twice.

I dressed like a fashion model instead of someone who pushed tokens and change. That particular night I'd worn a form-fitting, black two-piece pants outfit. It was hitting all the right notes and several passengers gave their complements with a nod or a thumbs up.

As usual, several of the cops teased me as though I was their little sister, while others thought they had a shot at something more. I didn't mind because as long as they were around, the Holdup Man wasn't. However, one Anti-Crime officer paid no attention to me at all. He sat quietly near the back of my booth on a stool with his eyes focused on every train and passenger coming through the station. He was very tall, extremely handsome with a few freckles and a mole on the side of his nose. The combination of freckles and a mole on his almond complexion looked sexy. When my 3 to 11 pm shift was over and the Anti-Crime unit prepared to leave, I did something out of character. After all, I was supposed to be chased not the one chasing.

"Okay guys," I announced, "I'll see you later."

After several enthusiastic goodbye hand waves, they exited the booth in single file. It seemed like a slow motion move as the quiet guy lifted off the stool. He pocketed his shift notepad and put his hand on the doorknob to leave.

"Excuse me, Mr. Quiet Guy," I mocked and slowly walked towards him. "What is your problem?"

He turned to me with a grin that appeared not only mischievous but somehow, intuitive. His brown eyes sparkled, and like a hypnotist holding me prisoner as if they were the handcuffs dangling from the side of his belt, I lost my ability to speak.

"My name is Rob," He began eyeing me from top to bottom, scanning my soul and my thoughts. "… and I don't have a problem, but you might if I don't leave right now."

Rob didn't leave. But from that same night, the only problem, if there was one, was my falling more in love with him and finding ways to show it.

Robert Walker, Jr., became my beauty for ashes.

"A merry heart doeth good like a medicine
but a broken spirit drieth the bones."
Proverbs 17:22 KJV

Chapter 10

As much as I went through with the wear and tear on my body and spirit, one of the gifts God gave me was laughter. Fortunately, God also had blessed me with someone who was just as spontaneous and comical.

One of the funniest moments Rob and I shared was on a date at a Red Lobster restaurant in the Green Acres shopping mall located in Queens, New York.

For a Saturday afternoon, it was more crowded than I'd seen before. Rob and I began laughing at the servers singing offkey a made-up Happy Birthday tune to an unfortunate birthday celebrator. The woman clutched her head, looked down and when she looked up, she appeared pale like they'd drawn all her blood.

Rob and I snickered. "Can you imagine being so embarrassed that you would have a complexion change?"

"Never gonna happen with us," Rob mumbled taking a bite from his biscuit and winking. "Plus, it would take a lot to embarrass us."

We were seated at a booth and immediately served with those delicious Red Lobster's Cheddar Bay biscuits and given a menu. The glossy pictured delights, many of which hadn't changed since Red Lobster sold seafood for the first time, showed a huge difference in our choices.

Rob would try anything once. I refused to consider anything hard to pronounce or that looked too foreign.

"We will have two orders of crab legs," he told the waitress as he flashed a smile at me.

The server, a young woman who looked exhausted, began writing and asked the usual follow-up question. "What will you have with that?"

"Hold up a minute," I told her. "I've never eaten crab legs," I told him through gritted teeth. "I want chicken. If that crab leg didn't start with feathers attached, I ain't eating it."

"You can have the baked potato," he teased. "Go easy on the butter if you still insist on fitting into that toddler size wedding dress you bought."

"You just keep that same smile and love when I fit into a size eighteen MuMu one day." I sucked my teeth and began turning to the page with the exotic virgin drinks.

"I most certainly will keep on loving you."

Turning back to the waitress, Rob said. "Thank you for your patience with my fiancée. With all that you've overheard please make it three orders of crab legs."

All I could do was laugh as the waitress continued trying not to join me in doing the same. I was ready to have a fun-filled battle. Rob was ready to eat.

About halfway through the meal after I'd scraped away all the potato leaving nothing but the skin, Rob insisted I try the crab legs.

He began with a bribe.

Cracking the leg, joint by joint, he dipped the meat in the butter and dangled it from a tiny two-prong fork. "You can have the final say on where we spend our honeymoon if you try just one tiny bite."

There was an unspoken rule between us. If either gets the upper hand—Go for broke.

I never saw it coming. I slowly pulled the crab meat off the fork with my tongue and the next thing I knew, I was blubbering like I was speaking in tongues.

In the loudest voice I could muster, I exclaimed, "Oh my goodness, Rob. I never had crabs until I met you!"

Red Lobster became pin drop quiet. It was as if —E.F. Hutton had spoken.

Rob dropped his head into his hands like an anvil was placed upon it. Meanwhile folks looked our way with mouths gaped.

—And I kept stripping the meat off the crab leg, dipping it in butter while letting the world know that I'd never had crabs until I met Rob.

Months later, on a beautiful Saturday in December, Rob married me anyway. I looked fabulous in my size six gorgeous white wedding gown while Arlene Smith sang, "At Last."

I always teased Rob that he didn't have much of a choice but to go through with the wedding. Who would want him after my crab declaration?

I've shared more shenanigans involving Rob and I in my eBook story, "Heaven Can Be Hell." Hawaii was hot for so many reasons. Just remember I wasn't always saved, and neither was Rob. Thank God for grace and mercy and a good sense of humor.

* * *

Rob and I were together for quite some time before I finally accepted the truth about our relationship. There was no other man with whom I'd want to spend my life. After the torment and betrayal from my first marriage, I was convinced that marriage was not for me, and I gave in. Instead of a small, informal wedding in the tiny apartment of a Church Mother, Rob and I were married in church. Rather than wearing an ugly two-piece suit, I wore a flowing, white pearl-covered gown with a long, embroidered train from "David's Bridal House," with a long floral-leaf veil. Rob's three brothers served as the best man and groomsmen. His young nephew and namesake, Robert, was the ring bearer.

I, on the other hand, had a maid of honor and matron of honor, along with two of Rob's nieces as junior bridesmaids and my goddaughter as my bridesmaid. My five-year old granddaughter was the flower girl. It was fabulous and unlike my first, Rob and I made all the decisions.

One of the other blessings resulting from my marriage to Rob was my family unit. Rob entered my life when my youngest daughter was almost four years old. The two older girls were ages nine and eight. A sample of God giving me beauty for my ashes was Rob's relationship with my daughters. Although, he never had children, he was hands-on. Whether it was the six nieces and nephews he helped his mother to raise or there was a need for his guidance, Rob answered the call.

During our thirty-six years of dating and marriage, he never once referred to the girls as "my stepdaughters." They were "my daughters." When the youngest graduated from nursing college, both Rob and Lee walked with her. There was never a time when Rob said anything negative about Lee to *our* girls. He was adamant that as young women, they could decide Lee's place in their lives. It was their choice if a man who wasn't a good husband could somehow still be a good father. And with Rob, there wasn't competition. If it was good for the girls, and Lee's involvement was needed, Lee was included.

As much anger as I had against Lee for the trials of our first marriage, it was the way Rob and he interacted that brought me around. We never became 'one big happy family,' and that was okay. We each had a role to play in making the adjustment to a peaceful co-existence, and so we did.

The other beauty was Rob's relationship with our grandchildren. To date, there are fourteen grandchildren and fourteen great-grandchildren. Strangely, the grands and the great-grands always, without wavering, considered Rob as their natural grandfather. They eventually learned of Lee's parental relationship to their mothers, but Grandpa Rob was the man they loved and honored.

***

Since the first time we met when he was an Anti-Crime cop, Rob went on to become a NYPD Detective, a NYPD/JTTF/FBI — (Joint Terrorist Task Force) Investigator on other "Special Assignments." Because he had unique skills involving interrogations and investigations, he was loaned to several Law Enforcement agencies. He was one of the JTTF's officers who brought in the pair of 1993 WTC bombers. He also helped solve the Queens Bombing case and several other high-profile crimes. He was a decorated Law Enforcement officer and recognized by then USAG (US Attorney General) Jo White.

There were other fun and less dangerous times during his career. Several of which because of my fondness for not taking things too seriously could've ended his promotions before they began.

Take for instance, when I attended my first FBI dance. As usual, with me, it was often "open mouth and insert foot." I was introduced to several FBI agents. Most of them looked like either Ms. Manners who wouldn't or couldn't hurt a fly or Mr. Robinson without the sweater.

The first words out of my mouth. "You all look so harmless. I'm certainly glad I didn't go into that life of crime like several of my cousins." I was on a roll. "By the way, where's Efrem Zimbalist, Jr.?"

If looks could kill—Rob's would've put me in an early grave. I'll always believe it was the laughter from the agents that saved me that night. I hadn't seen Rob that upset since the FBI interviewed me when he was up for another security clearance.

Me, being a jokester gave a crazy answer when the interviewer asked if Rob had any prejudices.

"Of course, he has prejudices."

When asked what it was, I offered, "He can't stand stupid people."

For the rest of our marriage, I always wondered when he'd dole out the "big payback."

He never did. At least I don't think he did. We just kept on loving and laughing.

As much as Rob accomplished in his Law Enforcement career, he was always one hundred percent supportive in whatever I chose to do.

One thing Rob and I didn't have in common was our choice of friends. I came to believe he was so *particular* in *who* he let enter his personal circle that it took a lot for him to accept some people, not necessarily 'friends' but associates on my journey.

For instance, on one occasion I was asked what notable or famous person I considered a friend; one who would surprise my readers.

I gave it some thought, and I must say it's probably former porn star, Vanessa Del Rio.

Pick your jaws up and let me explain.

When I worked for various record labels, there were huge entertainment conventions attended by a vast array of talent and stars.

One such function was held every year in Florida, and it was "must attend" to be seen and heard. 'Jack the Rapper' was also in attendance. This former radio DJ's unique style and charisma spawned a following of folks, from well-established record executives to major recording artists, as well as those from the film industry with a sprinkle of strippers, among others.

One afternoon during the conference, I entered a packed elevator, which held a woman in the corner surrounded by the convention press.

She looked familiar, and I concluded she was someone I probably watched on a soap opera. Eager to get off the humid elevator, I thought no more about it. However, it wasn't until a few hours later that I learned the gorgeous woman was the buxom porn star, Vanessa Del Rio.

After returning from the convention several days later, I was asked to attend a meeting at my NY attorney's office. Lo and behold, seated in one of the leather-backed chairs at a long cherrywood executive conference table was Vanessa Del Rio. It turned out we shared the same attorney. I'd barely gotten over that bit of trivia when I learned the purpose of the meeting was to try and shop a recording deal for her. Since I'd been successful with other artists I'd managed—I was chosen to bring forth this miracle.

A few days later, Vanessa and I met in Manhattan for lunch, to further discuss her ideas and the practicality of that venture. Once I got over who she was and how in the world this assignment fell into my lap, I found her to be very charming, engaging, and more intelligent than most of her admirers would've imagined.

I listened to the tape and promised I'd try my best. I knew obtaining a meeting with a Label Artist & Repertoire person would be easy based on *who* and *what* she was. However, I also knew getting them to take her seriously and take their minds out of the gutter might be a challenge. The track Vanessa recorded was looped with moans and groans, leaving nothing to the imagination and laying it all out on the bedspread. It was enough to make Donna Summer's 1970's disco hit, "Love to Love You" seem tame. The same track recorded by anyone else would've been easier to manage.

My effort turned out as I'd expected. However, I gained a friend. She once confided her regret at not having the kids and family she'd wanted. It was her choice to be in the porn business and her choice not to subject children to the ridicule. However, once she quit the XXX-rated film business, that move allowed her the time to pursue her other passion—photography and her newsletter.

Another incident involving Vanessa was the Geraldo Rivera Talk show. I received a fax requesting my help in securing an interview with her. The subject of the segment was "Porn Stars and What They're Doing Now." When I queried how the show acquired my contact information, I was told *Ron Jeremy*—another XXX-rated persona noted for the length of what hung below his belt rather than any knowledge claiming real estate above his neck—had provided it.

To be clear, I had never met nor spoken with Ron Jeremy in my life. It turned out my name was one of several Vanessa had given for contact purposes. It didn't matter. Vanessa was no longer in the business, and her appearance was no longer needed, but I won't say I wasn't peeved.

Except a few times since she made a cameo on NYPD Blue in 1996, I haven't spoken to Vanessa. However, I still have one of several gifts she gave us. It is a very expensive and beautiful pewter and pearl picture frame. As gorgeous as it is, her friendship remains one of the greatest gifts I've received and aside from being a friend and confidante, I'd done nothing to deserve it. My association came *judgement free*.

During my first marriage, I never experienced anything outside of the boundaries of housework, especially having friends of any sort, and when I tried, roadblocks sprang up like weeds.

* * *

There was a time when the show "The Twilight Zone" was looking for writers, and I had submitted a sample. A representative was sent to my Brooklyn, NY home. Lee immediately told the woman, "No." I never got through the interview process.

Another time was when an up-and-coming, playwright named William O'Neal had written a play called, "Quiet as It's Kept." He handed me a copy of his script, hoping I could compose its music. Lee tore it up right in front of Mr. O'Neal's face. Nothing but heated words flew instead of fists.

It took a while to let go of the anger. In my mind, Lee had destroyed any chance I had to realize one of my dreams—songwriting.

Only after I forgave and removed the hardness from my heart did God continue giving greater 'beauty for my ashes.' I went on to own two publishing companies with ASCAP® and BMI®.

Chapter 11

"True forgiveness is when you can say, "Thank you for that experience."

I have a friend and someone I consider, a sister, who is a Broadway star and television actress. Her name is Sandra Reaves-Phillips. Most people remember her as the music teacher in the film, "Lean on Me." I didn't get the opportunity to write the music for William O'Neal's play, "Quiet as it's Kept", but I was able to compose the title track for Sandra's "Heart to Heart" revue for the Village Gate in Manhattan. It was an honor and a small part of our musical journey together. Her other hit, among several, was her One-Woman show, "The Late Great Ladies of Music and Blues." She was and remains a phenomenal talent and extraordinary friend.

During the years I spent in the record industry; whether it was a part of the Doo Wop group, Arlene Smith and the Chantels, including singing on the Radio City Music Hall stage; working with Mr. James Brown, "Crazy" Wilson Picket, and so many other talented artists and traveling all over the country, Rob was there. When I went on to work in marketing and promotions with Columbia, Epic, and Def Jam Records, in or out of town, he was there in person or in spirit. Everyone knew and loved him, and very few knew he worked with the FBI.

Rob and I were huge Doo Wop fanatics. When the Chantels sang at Radio City Music Hall, Rob was in his element. Having one of his old Transit Police partners appearing on stage was almost too much for him. Emil Stucchio, Rob's old partner, led a group called the "Classics." They had a hit with their rendition of "Til Then." Rob strutted around backstage like he was the star. I'm surprised he didn't sign autographs. His wife and his old partner. What was not to brag about?

When I eventually began touring with my one-woman Christian comedy revue, "Sister Betty," he was front and center. The truth was that, if I missed any of my performances, Rob could've donned a wig and a Sister Betty costume and performed my entire routine.

Also, during that time, I wrote a twenty-two-page story based upon my show. My effort and what I'd learned about promotions from the record companies served me well. God took that little book that looked more like a pamphlet and turned it into a major, twenty-year publishing deal with Kensington/Dafina books. From that point on, I never had to do anything but write and perform. Success was what Rob wanted for me.

Chapter 12

Preach the word; be instant in season, out of season; reprove, rebuke, exhort with all longsuffering and doctrine.

2 Timothy 4:2 KJV

Later in our marriage, preaching and ministering to those in need was another thing Rob and I had in common. We loved the Lord. Rob could catch a crook in the morning and be behind the pulpit later that same day. Aside from preaching, he loved to pray.

Hungry? Did you want to hurry and eat? Rob was the one you did not want to bless the food when you were hungry. I would often tease him about praying so long that the gravy turned back into flour.

As much as his gun was a weapon, so much more was his Bible. Even now I enjoy pulling out one of his CD's and listening to him bring the Word or testifying. When I do, there is always something new to learn, and I feel as though I were seated on the front pew, proud and watching my Man of God glorifying a God he loved so much.

Making a choice to marry Rob at a time when I was so damaged was a miracle. Everything was out of the ordinary; from how we met to the moment he proposed. Perhaps, "proposed" is too strong a word. He came into the kitchen one afternoon. After supporting his chin with both palms, he simply said, "We need to do this."

In less than a year, we did just that. Rob was so romantic.

Although, I was *supposed* to have the final say on where we spent our honeymoon, of course, it was my fault we didn't have one. I was in the recording studio.

Weeks before our wedding, I'd been given a tape produced by an artist and producer I managed, who went by the name J. Dibbs. He'd penned hits for Vanessa Williams, Kenny Latimore, Brian McKnight, and others, to my former intern from Columbia Records, Brian Jackson. He'd gone on to become the Artist & Repertoire person at Mercury Records. In no time the track titled "I'm in Luv" was cut by R&B artist "Joe." No honeymoon for me and Rob, but a big hit for Joe. J. Dibbs and I also appeared in Billboard magazine and received a Worldwide EMI Pub deal, so it wasn't a total loss.

* * *

There were other tradeoffs and choices Rob and I made. While he solved the world's terrorist-related crimes, and dodged bullets during several shootouts, I scheduled promotional events for Epic, Columbia, and DefJam. I'd create or coordinate promotion efforts for other artists such as Regina Belle, Mariah Carey, Michael Bolton, 3rd Bass, and LL Cool J to name a few.

I had several favorites. Strange as it seems, it was the colorful and funny Flava Fav who made my day whenever he came to my office. He wore amazing colognes. The rap group, Nice and Smooth, were my babies. I loved their personas and sense of humor. Of course, there was LL Cool J. I am not surprised at his success at all. His mind for handling business was amazing. I adored Allyson "Just Call My Name" Williams. Her middle name will always be "Classy Gal" to me.

One of my highlights during that time was reuniting with Cheryl 'Pepsii' Riley when she recorded "Thanks for My Child." As a teenager, she had once recorded a demo at my Tomorrow's Sounds Demo Studio in Brooklyn.

Whether onstage or off, music remains one of my first loves.

"Whereas ye know not what shall be on the morrow. For what is your life? It is even a vapour, that appeareth for a little time, and then vanisheth away."

James 4:14 KJV

Chapter 13

Who would've believed a six-foot, three inch, almond-complexioned man, who praised God continuously all while he investigated and chased down terrorists, was the same man who broke down and sobbed inside the Downstate Neo Natal—NIC Unit in March of 2008?

Rob and I received news that our beloved newborn granddaughter, born at twenty-seven weeks, weighing less than two pounds, would not survive. That same proud man, with his chest heaving from crying, put one hand through the sleeve of the incubator and began praying.

With several tubes and IV's protruding from her tiny body, she grabbed Rob's pinky while he begged God to let her live. By the way she held onto his pinky, Rob then promised her that if she survived, he would survive the cancer that attacked his body.

That brave man was battling Multiple Myeloma cancer. He tried to share what little strength he had with his precious little granddaughter, Jonnay.

She survived and is a high-functioning, thirteen-year-old autistic, who excels in the arts, loves the Lord, and believes prayer is the answer to everything. Jonnay was introduced to prayer when she was born premature. She continues to honor God through praise dancing, singing, and her love for people and their needs. Every morning, she has Bible Study, often alone. Jonnay will not go to bed or get on the school bus without the two of us praying. I'd like to believe her spirituality mirrors what she's seen and heard from her beloved Grandpa Rob and me.

I pray she continues this path as a Chosen vessel for God.

* * *

One of the best lessons I learned from Rob while he battled cancer was how to trust God.

I remember the day we found out he had Multiple Myeloma. It was on his sixty-fifth birthday. He took it in stride.

I, on the other hand, became very angry. I wrote ten names on a yellow piece of paper. Those I felt were more deserving of this disease. To this day, I find it hard to believe I would do something like that.

Another characteristic of our marriage was honesty. We refused to lie to one another. However, when the oncologist revealed Rob had about eighteen months to live, I said nothing.

He fought so hard to live—the chemo, the radiation, stem-cell transplant and then he also had to go through dialysis three days a week.

Our finances took a huge hit. The cost for his chemo pills, Thalomid, came with a co-payment of anywhere from two thousand to four thousand dollars *a month*. We couldn't get help from Celgene, the manufacturer. Sometime later when Affordable Care (Obama Care) became available, that same prescription was lowered to one-hundred and eighty-five dollars per month. It angers me that but for God, we would not have been able to afford Celgene's exorbitant prices.

However, God kept us. Even though we'd lost almost one hundred thousand dollars from the 2008 bank fiasco, we never missed a mortgage or bill payment.

And then it was my turn to fight cancer.

Around 1997 while living in Queens, New York, I'd taken a biopsy in the office of a local GYN doctor. We soon moved and never received the results. I didn't give it a second thought.

In 2009, my GYN doctor ordered another painful biopsy. Shortly thereafter, I received a call to come to her office as soon as possible.

The gynecologist gave me the news. Oddly, I didn't react the same way I did when Rob's cancer was discovered. In fact, I was so nonchalant about it, she thought I was in shock.

I wasn't in shock at all. Surprised, yes. Rob was still battling his cancer and now we had mine to deal with.

A week after the diagnosis, the oncologist's office wanted to schedule surgery immediately. I informed him I had an upcoming performance for the next week and any surgery had to happen after that.

He thought I needed a psychiatrist instead of an oncologist.

However, Rob and I prayed. I gave it to God and had an amazing performance.

After surgery, there was no need for radiation, chemo, or even a pill. The oncologist was floored, and me too, when it was finally discovered that the cancer was originally discovered when I'd had the biopsy back in 1997. From 1997 to 2009, God hadn't allowed it to spread.

Sharing that journey with my Facebook followers was also a blessing. So many were going through similar health crises. I also learned what I'd experienced was never about me, but about God using me for His purpose and choice. It was the same with Rob. Had I not witnessed how he dealt with his cancer through his faith, I don't think I could've handled it.

Just as Rob had been given eighteen months to live, I was given approximately five years.

As of this date, I am in my twelfth year of cancer survival. I choose to live.

Rob lived on for seven years, the Biblical number of completion, before he passed.

The angels came to escort him to God in 2013. Most of that day, inside his hospital room, he and I had confessed our love to one another.

He said, "I'm going home today."

Because he was supposed to begin hospice care at home the next day, I thought that's what he'd meant. I had everything prepared, and the hospital bed and oxygen were supposed to be delivered later that evening.

With a weak voice, he and I sang songs of praise as I held his head in the crook of my arm. It was during that time when he asked, "Do you remember my covenant with God?"

I replied, "Yes."

"Say it," he remarked. "I want to hear you say it."

"Psalm thirty-seven and the twenty fifth verse," I replied. "I have been young, and now am old; yet have I not seen the righteous forsaken, nor his seed begging bread."

Rob slowly lifted his chin and declared. "God will keep His promise to me because I've kept mine to Him."

"I know He will," was my soft reply. "I'll be fine."

Rob had placed me in God's hands through his covenant, and I chose to believe as he did. He'd kept his promise to God, and the Covenant would be honored.

After a few moments, his legs thrashed about. His movements became violent, as though he were fighting the death angels who'd appeared to carry him away from me. It was then that I placed two fingers from my free hand on his wrist as his pulse slowed. When I looked down upon his face, the light left his eyes as they sank back, appearing vacant, never to gaze upon me again.

Seconds later, I kissed Rob's blue-tinged, ice-cold lips.

Rob left this earth, but his humor stayed behind. When I shopped for coffins, I'd picked out a very expensive one. As I was about to place the order with the funeral director, I heard Rob whisper, "You know that thing is going in the ground. Right?"

Immediately, I smiled and picked out an all-white casket. I could imagine Rob laughing, saying, "That's better."

* * *

Another beautiful part of my second marriage was that Rob did everything he could to make sure I had no pressure placed on me except to meet my publishing deadlines. That was my job—make the deadlines. I never worried about a bill or any of the household responsibilities.

Rob remained the jokester and protector to the end. He'd somehow managed to make the transition in my life from wife to widow as easy as possible. I believe there were times when he, without complaint, accepted his impending death and did what was needed, especially since I hadn't and wouldn't accept that he'd leave me.

Sadly, there was still a downside. When Rob passed away, I didn't know which bank held the mortgage on our house. Fortunately, he'd kept a small pad listing the websites, passwords, and other details pertaining to the upkeep of the house. He also made sure I was only listed as "authorized user" on the credit cards. It meant I was not responsible for any balances when he passed.

While Lee always tried to manipulate or minimize my income placed towards the upkeep, Rob made the opposite choice.

Oddly, several years after Rob's passing, Jonnay says she still remembers her beloved Grandpa Rob waving to her from outside her window. She was only five when she last saw him alive and was in preschool on that day. Yet she describes him as wearing "a blue gown."

Jonnay says she speaks to him often. "Grandpa says he's cold and wants to come inside."

I cannot pretend to understand their bond. However, when Rob passed, he was wearing a blue hospital gown. His precious five-year-old grandbaby was not there. I may not understand, but how can I not believe her?

Seven years later, my heart and I still had not written much, except for a couple of eBooks. My performances were almost nonexistent. I didn't have it in me. It was as if when Rob left, he'd snatched my love for writing comedy with him.

Laughing too much, enjoying life too much seemed dishonest and unfaithful to a man I still loved beyond the grave.

I attended a wake for one of my brothers-in-law who passed after Rob. One of his friends touched my hand, and I almost cried. Even another man touching me for no purpose other than to say "hello," or "how are you doing?" made me feel unfaithful. I was a mess. I'd chosen to go on while still messed up.

A few months ago, on a Saturday around mid-morning, I heard Rob's still voice say, "Take me out of your mind, but keep me in your heart. Move on and fulfill your purpose. Choose better.

You don›t spend half your life with someone who was perfect for you without missing them in a mighty way. It was as though while God was creating Rob, he had asked, "Pat, my child. What do you want in a man? In a husband?"

"Make him faithful," I imagine, I told God. "Not only faithful to me but faithful to you, Father God. Let the two of us be of one mind. Can you please add in a little wisdom to show he can be completely loving to my body, as well as my mind? And if it wouldn't be too much, can you make him wise with our finances? Lord, you know I'm a shop-a-holic."

A peace came over me on Saturday, January 16th. Not a calmness that I can describe. How can there be a peace that saturates your entire being, breaking chains of grief that once held you as though they were made of steel? How can there be contentment intertwined with every thought and memory, waking moment, and restless night? Every song I'd heard over the past seven years was our song. In public, couples smiling, holding hands without shame, was us. Even secret and coded gestures from these strangers became what I'd had with Rob.

* * *

I am finally beginning to write again. After all, I may be an Essence® and National bestselling author, but my choice is to fulfill God's purpose for my life. My supporters have been so patient. Seven years late. Seven is the biblical number that represents completion, and so I must do as my beloved husband ordered from his spiritual world. I must get him out of my head and make room for my creativity to flow again. I will forever keep him in my heart.

Rest in peace, my beloved husband Rob. I'll see you on the other side.

Author's Note

You stood in the gap. Interceded on behalf of someone or something. However, what you prayed was what you thought was needed. Perhaps, it took a moment, but you later learned, sadly, with all your good intentions and spiritual insights, you might have stood in God's way.

For example, someone you knew and loved constantly chose the wrong path. You bailed them out, gave them a place to lay their head, and your blood pressure soared. You prayed repeatedly. Nothing you did worked—until you finally threw up your hands, moved out of the situation and truly gave it to God to have His way.

Yet, on the other hand, some are anointed with the gift of a fervent prayer life. They are often called Prayer Warriors. Moses "stood in the gap and petitioned God on behalf of the Israelites." His special prayer saved the people of Israel. However, he was chosen to do so. (Psalms 106:23)

Accept that there is a difference between choosing to pray God's Will and making a choice to pray Yours.

Why?

God's purpose for our lives will be impacted by our choices when we think we know more than Him. We don't, and it's foolish to believe that we do—If we come to a crossroad where a choice must be made, it is wise to create "that choice" at the foot of the Cross.

Black Steel

by Pat G'Orge-Walker © 1999

Struggles, they attacked me
Though I had no permanent shape
They found me and when they did
I was thrust into a fire
And without my permission
I was shaped and hammered in that fire
Only to be quickly submerged in cool water

Often, certain blessings came upon me
And when I gave no thanks
Without a second thought, I was
Thrust again into the fire
Hammered and reshaped
Again, quickly submerged in cool waters

At an age where knowledge should have ruled me
Instead, I searched for more comfortable things
To use as my consequence, again into a fire
Chastised with life's repercussions and reshaped
Once more, then quickly submerged in cool waters

After repeated lessons, good and bad
After being consumed over and over in the fire
I became hard, impossible to break,
My spirit soared with invincibility

"Now I see" said my reason for being
Black Steel only comes about
After the thrusting in many fires
And the cooling off in many waters
I have arrived, I am ready for warfare
I am a supernatural weapon
I am God's Black Steel
Only to bend and to be used
by His Will

Pat G'Orge-Walker is the *Essence*, *USA TODAY* and National bestselling and award-winning author of the Christian fiction Sister Betty comedy series, as well as contemporary fiction, Women's issues, Romance novels. The novels published by Kensington/Dafina that fearlessly burrow into issues sometimes labeled taboo or left unsaid by Christian and secular community without subverting the Good News or watering down the potency of its message. She is also a contributor to New York Times anthologies and a three-time AALAS winner for Comedy as well as several other prestigious awards.

Pat, a PK, has quietly soaked up material from her father's Baptist congregation and her mother's Pentecostal assembly to create and keep her audiences howling with laughter, performing nationwide and on the high seas with her One-Woman comedy show, "Sister Betty! God's Calling You!"

Before entering the Publishing arena, she was a recording industry veteran working promotion/marketing with Epic, Columbia and Def Jam records. And, before that, she sang with Arlene Smith and the Chantels (Maybe, He's Gone, Look in My Eyes.)

Today, she is constantly looking to connect further with her reader and fan base. The First Lady of Gospel Comedy forges a successful career as author and comedian. She currently resides in NC. Find her on the web and social media: Pat G'Orge-Walker www.pgorgewalker.com

The Merry Hearts Inspirational Series will touch your soul and warm your heart

Heaven Foxx thought she was on top of her game until she meets the Rev. Averic Domingo; a young man handsome enough to grace the cover of a fashion magazine but much too attached to his pulpit. The good Reverend preached against having any type of kinky sex in or out of the bedroom until Heaven walked into his life. She is hell bent on showing him just how wrong he had been. They both have met their match in one another and have a lot to lose when they find out ... Heaven Can Be absolute Hell!

Chapter 1

Averic's head snapped upward at the annoying static sound that snatched him from preparing for his sermon.

"Be warned; all verified hell is about to visit you," Aunt Peaches blasted from the intercom.

"Say what?" Startled, the six-foot-five, thirty-five-year-old shot forward in his chair. The sudden movement caused him to scrape his knee against the side of the desk. He grimaced at the sudden bite of pain as he pressed the intercom's button. "Say that again."

Being out of breath and inhaling quickly caused a slight hiccup to escape in her excitement. She blurted in her signature rapid-fire and politically incorrect manner, "Well, nephew-pastor, it's a warm and lovely May afternoon, and I know you studying so you can preach everybody to Paradise come your turn next Sunday morning, especially since you figuring you gonna become senior pastor in a few weeks—"

Averic sighed his frustration. For a while, rumors were going around the church and town that his gossipy widowed aunt was looking for a new husband. Aunt Peaches, built like a rusty-colored beer keg, was seen in some of her pre-saved life hangouts trying to use her old fleshly equipment as unwanted collateral. He didn't want her feelings hurt or someone getting shot, since she was also a licensed concealed gun carrier. Feeling obligated, Averic hired her to be his assistant. And that's when the real fun began.

Today, he had promised to meet with Pastor's Aid Committee heads Mama Mae-Aye and Trustee Black Mack to discuss the upcoming retirement benefit for the current senior pastor. *I might as well pull out the checkbook. They're gonna tell me how cheap I am and that five thousand dollars couldn't buy a decent tablecloth.* He was sure that the Lord himself popped Tylenol every time those two old shysters complained. However, he still didn't appreciate his aunt's reference.

"Let me remind you again," Averic said slowly, still massaging his sore kneecap, "I don't want you comparing any meeting I have with our members to a session in Hell."

The sound of a small, exasperated gasp filtered through the intercom. Aunt Peaches lowered her voice, adding in a more respectful, yet reprimanding tone, "Well please forgive me, Wanna-be-a-Senior Pastor-elect-Reverend-Doctor-Averic Domingo. As your late mama's only sister and your once-favorite auntie, I was just tryin' to tell you that Mama Mae-Aye and Trustee Black Mack can't make their scheduled meeting."

"Seriously?" He could have stayed home and packed for his upcoming trip instead of traipsing across town to the church to get his feelings hurt in what was sure to be a geriatric beat down.

A chuckle quickly replaced the stern measure in Aunt Peaches' voice. "Actually, I overheard a conversation while I was in the second stall in the second-floor ladies' room."

Averic slapped a hand to his forehead harder than he had meant to. The devil is a liar. The last thing he wanted was that mental picture to accompany his aunt's confession.

"Ain't no secret that all kinds of truths and such can be learned from any second stall in the ladies' bathroom all over the world," she said, oblivious to the fact that she was making lunch an impossible thing. "Like I said, they're gonna go over to Shout Now Community Church for their Elders' Day celebration this evenin'."

"Thank you for all your extra info," Averic replied slowly, knowing from past conversations during Thanksgiving dinners, barbecues, and every other family-related occasion that it would be fruitless to remind her of her fondness for giving too much information. Instead, he replied, "Well, since they canceled and we've discussed not having any hellish meetings," he paused, making certain his point still carried, "and I don't have another meeting scheduled this afternoon, I'm leaving so I can get to the airport and make it to the Annual Honolulu Singles and Married Couples retreat in Hawaii for the next few days."

As a further reminder that she should not have tacked something else on his schedule, he added, "I hope to meet with Minister Craig during his Couples Retreat function."

"Hold up, I wouldn't exactly say you don't have any other

meetings today," Aunt Peaches told him in a manner that suddenly sounded a bit more serious than necessary.

Averic froze in the middle of returning his documents to a manila folder. "What do you mean?"

"I mean, you can't go home because now you do have another meeting." Her high-pitched nasal voice returned as she cautioned, "It's someone who hasn't been here in a while. I guess she's overdue for a visit."

Peaches' voice betrayed her as a sudden snicker came over the intercom, masking her mocked concern.

Averic's eyes rolled in pure frustration. "Well, whoever she is, I don't have time to meet with her. I'm certainly not in the mood for any confusion right now. Let one of the deacons deal with whatever problem she has."

"Deacon Slipp," Aunt Peaches blurted. "He seen her first and he passed the word onto me. He may be about my age, but he's too old for this new-fangled mess younger folk bringing to the church. He said he knew trouble when he seen it and his power of discernment had told him that he wasn't missing no five-dollar Mighty Wing special at Church's Chunky Chicken to handle it."

The loud sound of Aunt Peaches' wheezing echoed. "So, it looks like you'd better make time, and as much as it pains me to say it, you gotta take a hit for the church's sanity team. Besides, you supposed to stay prayed-up." She lowered her voice. "I'd stay and sit in this particular meeting with you, but I ain't that saved yet."

Aunt Peaches' sometimes-zany remarks still managed to catch him off guard, but admitting something like that last part put him on notice. His nose twitched as though he could smell the always pleasant aroma of his Acqua Di Gio cologne fading, his plane ticket to Hawaii for three days disappearing into volcanic smoke, and the acrid smell of Hell's sulfur permeating the office air.

"Okay," he snapped. "Send whoever she is in here. It's my charge to keep. Who is it?"

"Glad you finally got around to asking because she's waiting inside the sanctuary. You ain't seen that heffa in a long time. I hoped you'd never see her again."

Choosing to ignore Aunt Peaches' devilish reference to someone being a "heffa," he replied, "Well, bring her inside, please. I really want to get out of here as soon as possible."

"Not as soon as you'll wanna be," Aunt Peaches replied angrily. "because it's your wife. I still can't figure out why her mama named that hellion Heaven."

Smooth-talking Musician, Sanjay Thomas' "hit it and quit it" past has caught up to him. Like a Mack truck, it will flip him and leave him waffling, wondering if Jesus was only kidding about forgiving him. Falling in love with best selling author, Celeste Francois, was unplanned. That romance placed him in a situation where a 'lie' will force him to make another life-altering decision; if he leaves her, he will save Celeste's fragile self-esteem and her amazing literary career from being destroyed, staying is no longer an option. Sanjay Thomas makes the sacrifice to abandon her ... but for how long?

Celeste Francois, a single mother with a pair of ten year-old high-spirited twin girls, Jonnay and Jeannette, is on a mission. Celeste is seeking revenge on the man who told her he didn't care if she thought she was overweight. He didn't care if she was more successful in her writing career than he was as a struggling musician. He said he just wanted her for her. She knew he lied when he suddenly disappeared without a word. .

Nothing has prepared her for the shock of learning the object of her hatred will return from the shadows fifteen years later until the church hires him to be the musical director for the Masterpiece she works hard to put in production. Now she's mad and conflicted enough to think she can persuade Jesus to let her have revenge on the man who's turned her world upside down, after that they can go their separate ways. Celeste brings her own brand of hell to Sanjay. Heaven help him, he's going to need it.

Chapter 1
Celeste Francois

Unlike the pigeons that happily pecked at crumbs on the dirty sidewalk below her apartment, Brooklyn's own unlucky pigeon, Celeste Francois, felt like a hostage. For several years, she'd been tied and strangled by the ropes of poverty. She had given in to believing she'd never leave that New York borough and become a dove.

She'd been awake since the sun came on duty earlier, still lying across her full-size bed, summoning all her overweight ancestors to come to her aid.

While the weather outside was warm and welcoming that morning, inside Celeste Francois' tiny apartment, a storm was brewing.

"I am more than a conqueror," she told herself. Unfortunately, no amount of self-convincing or hypnotism in the world could conquer all her belly fat. She found ways to camouflage it over the past nine years, off and on, by wearing the latest late-night 'Get-Skinny-Quick' gimmick that never worked. Her daily routine consisted of trying to cram her pounds of the post-pregnancy fat into a pair of plus size jeans.

"This don't make no doggone sense," she pined, groaning with all the effort. "I just bought these a month ago." She rolled her eyes to the ceiling while thinking of a million other things she'd rather do on her thirty-fifth birthday.

"Mama, please hurry. We're hungry."

The plea came from her ten year-old identical twins, Jeannette and Jonnay, her mini-me opinionated girls. When they weren't working her nerves, she did everything to spoil them. She had very little, but was filled with determination to give the pair of energetic, coffee-colored, four-foot ninety pounds of pig-tailed, dawn-to-evening questioning kids, the love and attention she'd never received from her parents.

Looking away from Celeste, the twins twisted their lips trying to hide the sneer they knew might bring them closer to a threat of a spanking than they'd want.

Under her steely gaze, they swallowed their comments but glanced at each other. With complaints silently shared—a twin-thing they'd learned at a young age—they continued struggling to balance a huge box between them.

The twins had remained silent, but it didn't stop Celeste from ranting as though she'd read their minds. "Will you two just stop aggravating me?" Celeste snapped. Sweat popped from her forehead as she motioned to herself. "You two see I'm trying to get dressed."

Jeannette, a bit older than her twin by almost three minutes, replied dryly, "Ain't nobody trying to aggravate you, Mama. One of them moving men say they done you a favor even coming here yesterday and today. He said he's gonna just put the rest of your 'crappy' stuff back on the truck." She took a deep breath. "He say he's gonna drive off if you don't pay them the rest of they money."

Jeannette quickly lifted her chin and nodded at her twin. "Didn't he say that, Jonnay?"

Jonnay, following her sister's lead as always, sighed. "He sure did." Her hands jerked as she shifted her end of the box, filled to the top with her mama's good dishes. "And I'm getting tired."

Celeste moaned, and stared at the ceiling. She grimaced, and then set her face in a determined mask despite the pain.

Maybe it was tiredness that made Jonnay forget her second-place status. She went full rogue and wasn't through complaining.

"That other man," she began, "the one smelling like a skunk wearing bad vanilla—like you always say when somebody is stinking—said that 'cause you went out a time or two wasn't enough reason to let you slide on the rest, Mama." She sped up to get the rest of her report out. "He was even winking like something was in his eyes when he said to tell you that. And then he said, real loud, like he wanted everybody outside to hear, that y'all can discuss it like y'all used to." She hunched her shoulders adding, "Whatever that means."

"Yeah, but¬—" Jeannette chimed in. "That other man with those black ashy ears like a homeless bunny rabbit said there wasn't gonna be no discussion. Just pay him his—" she frowned. "He said a bad word—money."

Defeated, Celeste lowered her head to her chin. Struggling, Celeste threw her head back onto the pillow. "C'mon now." She gritted her teeth. Her hips bobbed like two overripe cantaloupes with stretch marks. "Finally," she announced as the jeans made its way to her waist without getting anything caught in its zipper.

Celeste slid off the side of the bed and didn't so much as blink. She gestured with a flip of one hand, ordering, "Sit it in the corner next to the refrigerator." Then, she slipped into a pair of house shoes that once had two-inch heels. Over time, her weight had turned them into a pair of no-inch flats.

Jonnay scanned the room, then looked at her sister as though waiting for Jeannette's approval to speak. Her brown eyes narrowed as she inquired, "Mama, where's the rest of the kitchen? When we got here last night, I thought it was bigger."

"Yeah, Mama," Jeannette, added. "The last three places we lived we didn't have to walk out of it and turn around to get to the stove." She tossed the question to her sister. "Ain't that right, Jonnay?"

Jonnay nodded. "Didn't have to think about opening the fridge first to get inside the oven or the other way round, too."

Celeste frowned at the girls, resting her hands on her massive hips. Her head swung between them, giving each the old Southern Mama's 'evil eye'.

The girls gulped and swallowed whatever words were on the tip of their tongues as they trotted away to do as they were ordered.

Celeste hung her head, whispering a prayer. "Lord, how long do I have to live like this? Can I at least catch a break on my birthday?" Not waiting for an answer, or truly expecting one, she opened the door and waddled down to the steps from her one-bedroom, third-floor walk-up apartment.

"Those girls deserve better than this," she whispered. "It doesn't make no sense I need to keep moving because I don't always have the rent." Winded, she stopped and rested against a wooden bannister for a moment.

Two flights down to go and two angry men awaited; one wanting money, the other want "something" more. Celeste simply wanted some peace of mind and a better life for her girls. And, if life would finally be so kind, she'd also like to get her hands around Sanjay Thomas' neck and send him to meet his maker.

Chapter 2
Sanjay Thomas

Many New York residents struggled to survive, but not in Sanjay Thomas's world. Life was getting better everyday in almost every way. Except two things—Al Green's famous love and happiness.

Inside his spacious five-bedroom, three-and-a-half bath home—complete with manicured grounds and a huge two-car garage situated in the posh area of Westchester County, New York—he whispered, "God, thank you for being the God of second chances."

Sanjay shook his head, as he'd done often, at how far he'd come in the past year alone. The smooth sounds of Richard Smallwood's 'Angels Watching Over Me' echoed from the Bose system. He scooted back onto his leather pit sectional sofa and gave an audible sigh while scanning his surroundings. His lavish ivory-and-taupe living room was equipped with Cathedral windows that stood open to let in the cool night air.

He leaped off the sofa, clasping his fingers together and forming a temple before lowering his head. In submission, he stood before a large, expensive oil painting of Jesus. The picture hung above a white, marbled fireplace overlooking several awards for his gold and platinum gospel compositions displayed across its mantle. Sanjay's broad shoulders swayed as thoughts that wavered between gratefulness and loneliness nearly overwhelmed him. After all, with so many blessings raining down on him, a forty-something year-old man shouldn't cry. Besides, a pair of bloodshot and puffy eyes wouldn't look good on the cover of Today's Inside Gospel magazine.

Finally, looking up and exhaling, Sanjay checked his two-thousand-dollar IWC Portugieser Automatic watch with its legendary Pellaton winding system and ceramic components. *Father God, I'm still conflicted. Perhaps, I shouldn't have accepted such an extravagant gift from the Board of Bishops.*

Yet, he had, especially when the board explained, "You've put our congregation on the map. Every concert, conference, or play we've produced over the past fifteen months has been phenomenal and financially successful. And if we preach prosperity, then our ministry needs to look prosperous. You're going to be on the cover of a famous gospel magazine. You can't be wearing some cheap, on-sale watch from Amazon."

Would the Board feel that way if they knew the truth about him? That question haunted Sanjay because they didn't know his entire testimony. Sanjay had wanted to tell them on so many occasions. He'd wanted to confess how his past wasn't always pretty. Once he overcame homelessness and other pitfalls of life, he didn't want to remember any of those ugly experiences. Every success stabbed his conscience despite the words of gratitude that spewed off his tongue. Sanjay was convinced God would place him in a situation where he'd have no choice but to tell it all. "Thank you, Lord, for new mercies every day," he whispered.

So far, he hadn't been exposed, but that didn't stop him from looking over his shoulder while holding a glimmer of faith.

Twenty minutes later, the camera crew snapped pictures of him in various poses around the living room. Thankfully, the interview didn't take long. The female journalist, who wore a form-fitting dress that left nothing to anyone's imagination, asked the same questions as all the other entertainment papers. When she kept smoothing her dress or pursing her lips when she spoke, Sanjay instantly picked up that she was a bit more flirty than professional. Also apparent, was the fact that his now burgeoning size didn't matter. He had the three "F"s some women liked ... Fame, Fortune, and Flash. So they could overlook a few extra pounds. Thankfully, it was only a few and he could get back to his regular size if he put the effort into it.

He'd smiled and played it safe by giving Sanaa Lucas details of his obligatory made-up past. Sanjay scattered in enough distorted facts to blame the magazine if his answers proved false or his past was discovered. As hard as he'd prayed for forgiveness, his pride always interfered. Either way, he never revealed his complete history to anyone.

"I can't thank you enough for this wonderful opportunity and blessing," Sanjay smiled at the attractive columnist from Today's Inside Gospel magazine as he escorted her and the crew outside. "It didn't take too long for you to get me to spill everything," he teased, knowing she'd been able to do anything but.

"You were an excellent interviewee," she replied, running a hand through her silky weave for the umpteenth time. "Can I call you directly if I need any further info?"

"I certainly hope I've given you all you need." Sanjay spoke slowly, hoping she understood there wouldn't be a follow up. Just in case he wasn't clear, he added, "I'm about to go back into my creative cave and write. It's how I stay on top. I hope you understand."

If she understood, she said nothing. Pushing one of the crew aside, she hurried inside the van but not before glaring over her shoulder at Sanjay. Then, a false smile appeared on her ruby-red lips when she looked at him again. A shiver of unease slithered up his spine.

Back inside his home, Sanjay pondered what had just gone down and the real or perceived threat of being discovered by the female reporter who hadn't accepted 'not interested' as an answer.

Sure, he was riding high now, yet eleven years ago he couldn't have caught a ride in a three-wheeled shopping cart. Back then, he had two patched shirts, two pairs of dark-colored pants, and a pair of shoes that had seen the inside of an old shoe repair shop more than the shop's resident roaches.

Things hadn't always been that way. The year before he'd joined the near-homeless population, he'd co-written a song for a chart-topping album. Being dumb and naïve, he'd practically given away most of his publishing rights to his co-writer, Jackson Lamont, and settled for a big advance. He never dreamed his song would be nominated for a Grammy. It didn't win, but he received the necessary recognition for his efforts He did have a problem, though. He'd spent that advance money on wine and women and never got around to writing another song. His bedroom had a revolving door, letting women in and out within an hour or two. Sometimes, he hadn't bothered to get their names or ages. What he should've been doing was revolving his butt on that piano bench and cranking out another hit or two.

Despite the dwindling finances, he played one expensive game too many. His life took a downward plunge on the night he decided to play fast and loose with Celeste Francois, an upcoming successful romance writer.

They'd met fifteen years ago during a meet and greet for her latest book, Mediterranean Rhapsody, at the Lavish Publishing Company party in downtown New York City. He was low on money and had returned to gigging. That night, he put aside his anger at what Jackson had done, and tucked away the jealousy that Jackson had succeeded on the strength of Sanjay's creativity. As an olive branch, Jackson reached out to him and extended an offer for Sanjay to play piano with a five-piece Ska-Rock Funk band that Jackson managed.

Once Sanjay realized that Celeste was a popular and famous author—on a level where he was once as a songwriter—he'd felt a sense of kinship. Sanjay hadn't meant for things to go as far as they did. He felt comfortable in her presence that night and he dismissed his normal preferences. Celeste weighed about thirty pounds more by his standards. He'd always preferred a female who looked more like a cover girl than one who needed covering up.

After sharing several mixed drinks and nibbling at the food, the conversation turned more personal. She'd loosened up a bit and was more talkative than he had been since he was keeping his eye on Jackson who had a tendency to skip out with the cash, forcing band members to hunt him down to get their money.

"I've never been married," Celeste had shared. "Barely have opportunities for dating with writing and making deadlines taking up so much time."

"I can certainly appreciate that," he'd told her, half-heartedly.

He remembered the feeling of disappointment after she'd said that and wishing he appreciated that fame could be fleeting. If he'd done like Celeste, he would've gone on to possibly playing at Radio City Music Hall with a second shot at a Grammy.

Instead, there he sat at a book release party, having swallowed his pride and working gigs for his shady writing partner. Jackson, the same backstabbing predator he had blamed for costing him a Grammy, introduced him to underground parties where so much wickedness went on, Sanjay was repenting simply for the things he'd seen, and not anything he'd done.

"I can't totally blame Jackson," Sanjay whispered, stroking a hand over a Stellar Award that he'd won earlier that year. "I should've fought harder for what I wanted."

Including Celeste Francois.

While his unsuccessful past played in his mind, as it often did these days, Sanjay strolled down the hallway toward his master bedroom. He stopped abruptly and looked into one of the many sculptured mirrors hanging throughout his home. His body stiffened as if it were a statue as he peered deep into the mirror. Sanjay had no control and his mind won the battle of remembering that night. He recalled the moment when he'd felt closer to Celeste than any other woman he'd been with before. As hard as he tried to forget, Sanjay remembered every word of their conversation.

The loss of her meant Sanjay Thomas had gained the world, but she still held a small part of his soul.

Pat G'Orge-Walker's
AUTHOR CATALOG

For more info visit

www.pgorgewalker.com